AHIAHIA

THE ORPHAN

Published by Inhabit Media Inc.
www.inhabitmedia.com

Inhabit Media Inc. (Iqaluit) P.O. Box 11125, Iqaluit, Nunavut, X0A 1H0

Design and layout copyright © 2022 Inhabit Media Inc.
Text copyright © 2022 Levi Illuitok
Illustrations by Nate Wells copyright © 2022 Inhabit Media Inc.

Translator: Jeannie Illuitok
Editors: Neil Christopher, Anne Fullerton, and Kelly Ward
Art Director: Danny Christopher
Designer: Sam Tse

This project was made possible in part by the Government of Canada.

We acknowledge the support of the Canada Council of Arts for our publishing
program.

Printed in Canada

Library and Archives Canada Cataloguing in Publication

Title: Ahiahia the orphan / by Levi Illuitok ; illustrated by Nate Wells.
Names: Illuitok, Levi, author.
Identifiers: Canadiana 20220245568 | ISBN 9781772274431 (hardcover)
Subjects: LCGFT: Picture books.
Classification: LCC PS8617.L58 A73 2022 | DDC jC813/.6—dc23

AHIAHIA

THE ORPHAN

BY **LEVI ILLUITOK** · ILLUSTRATED BY **NATE WELLS**

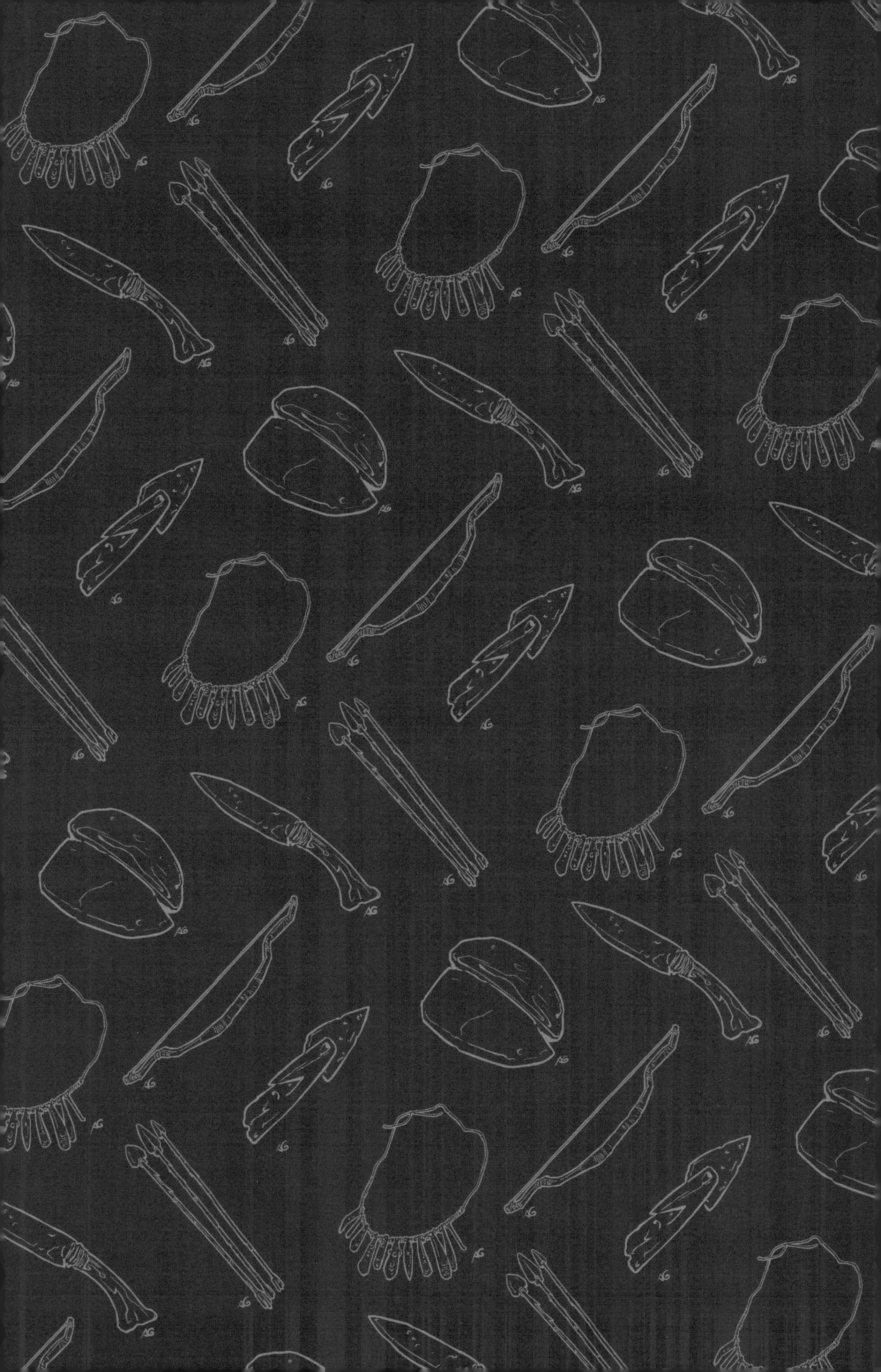

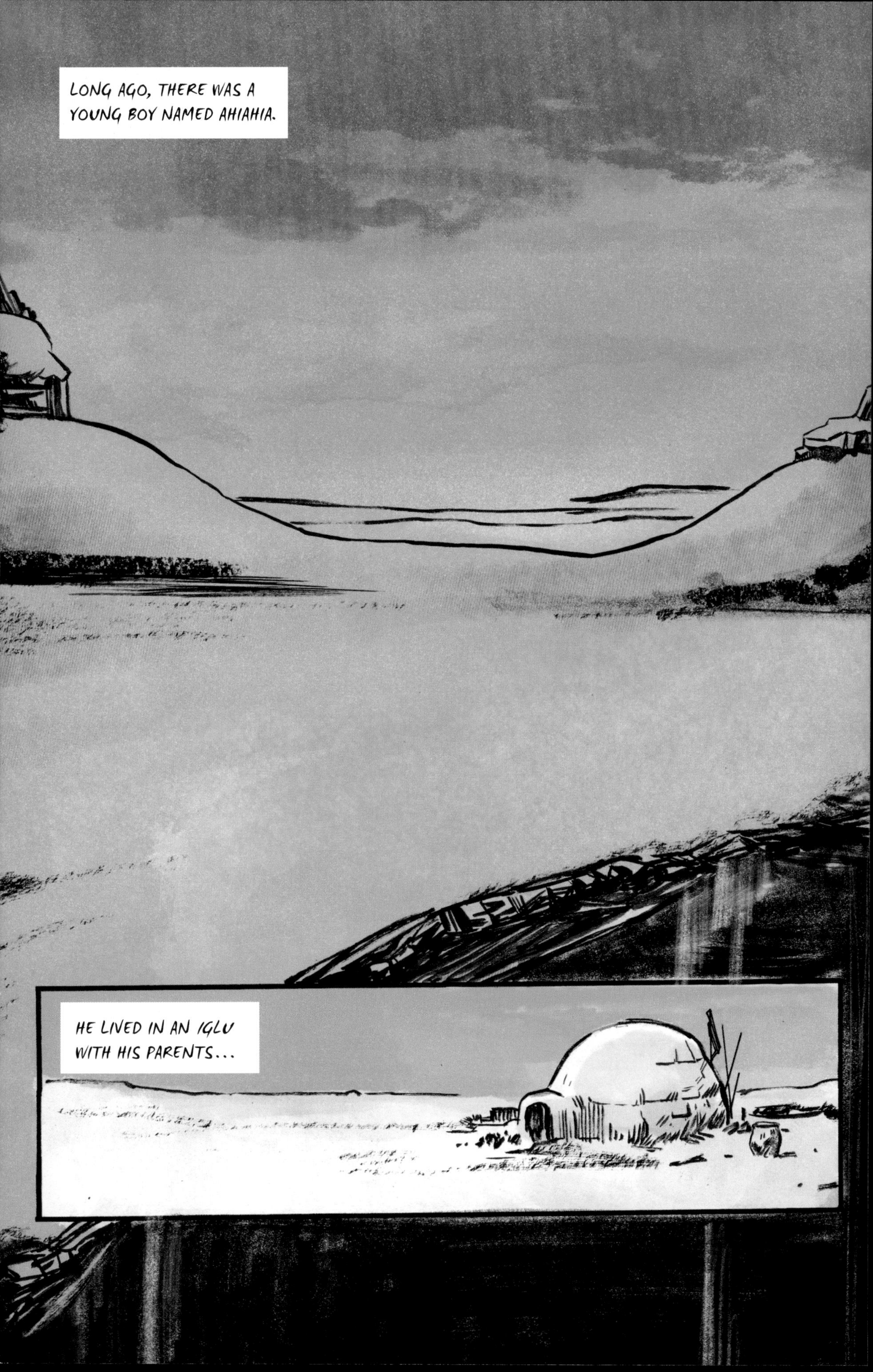
LONG AGO, THERE WAS A YOUNG BOY NAMED AHIAHIA.
HE LIVED IN AN IGLU WITH HIS PARENTS...

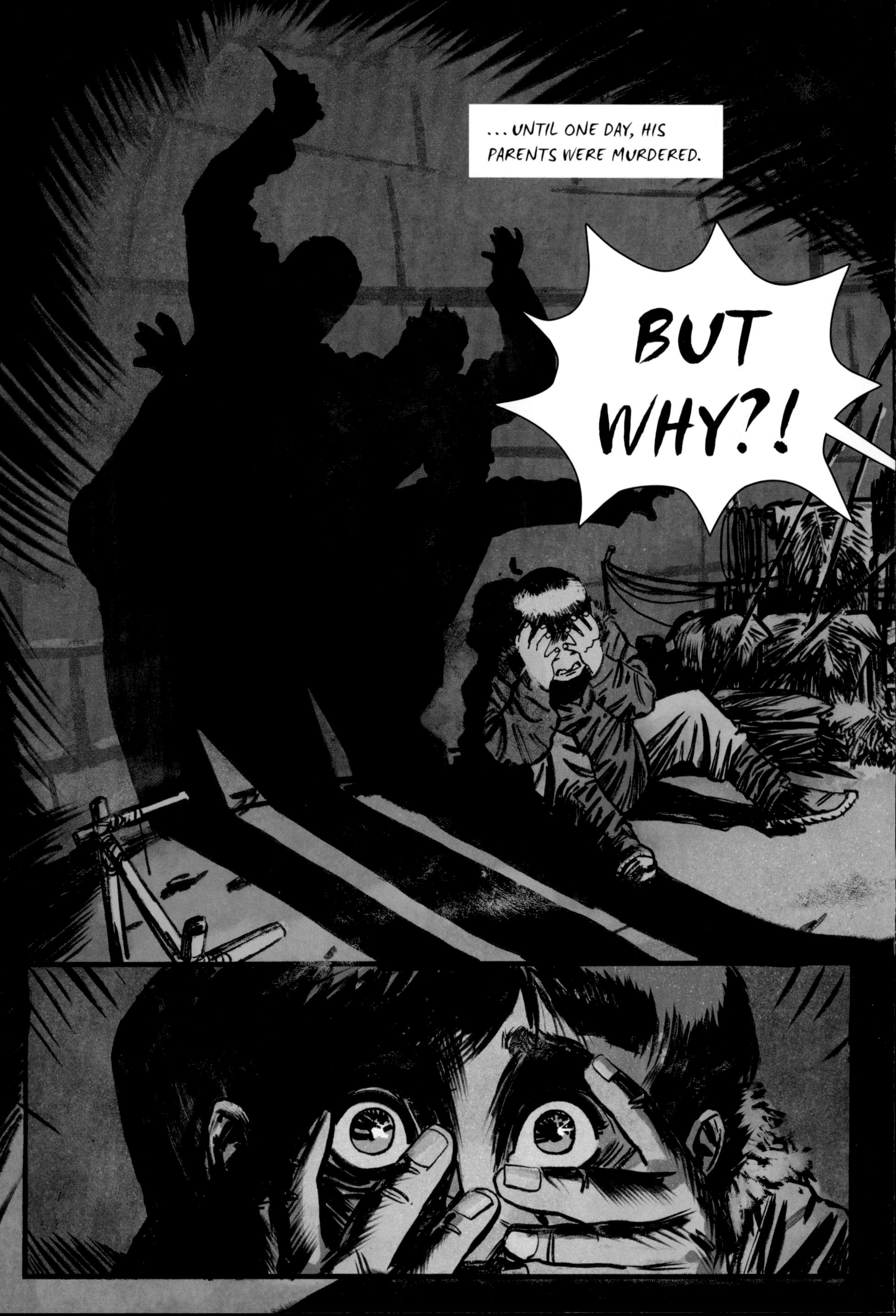
...UNTIL ONE DAY, HIS PARENTS WERE MURDERED.
BUT WHY?!

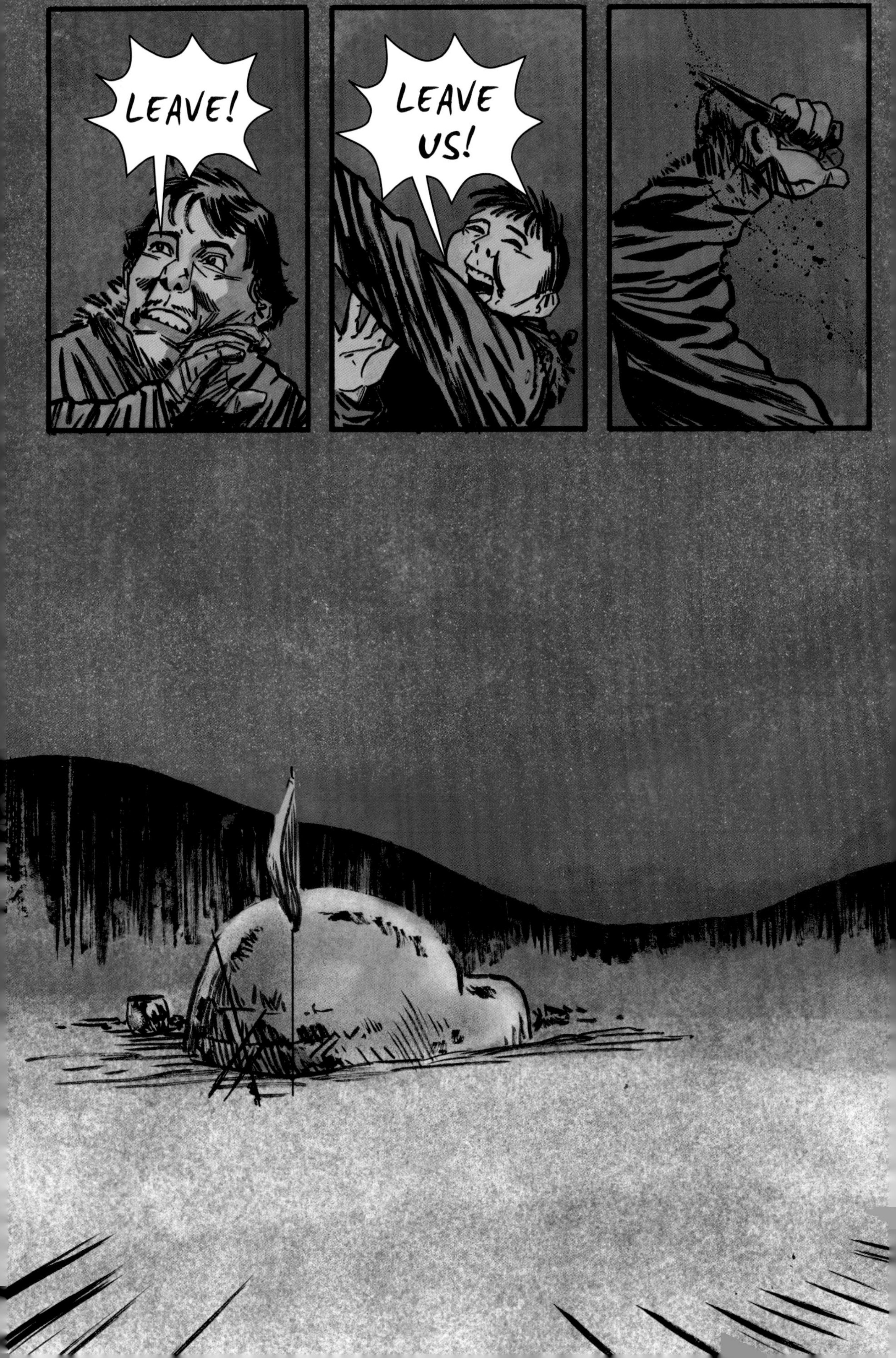
LEAVE!
LEAVE US!

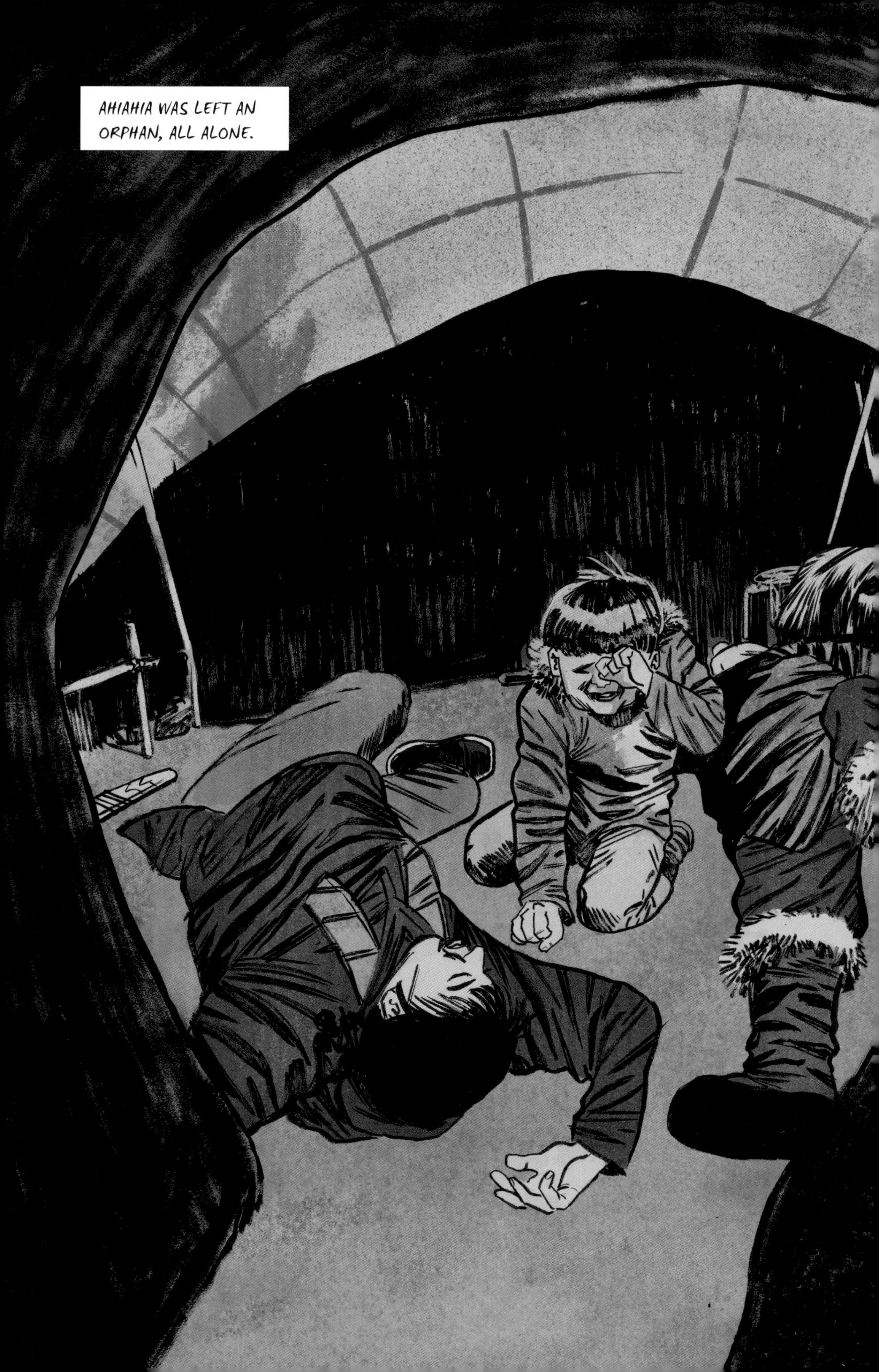
AHIAHIA WAS LEFT AN ORPHAN, ALL ALONE.

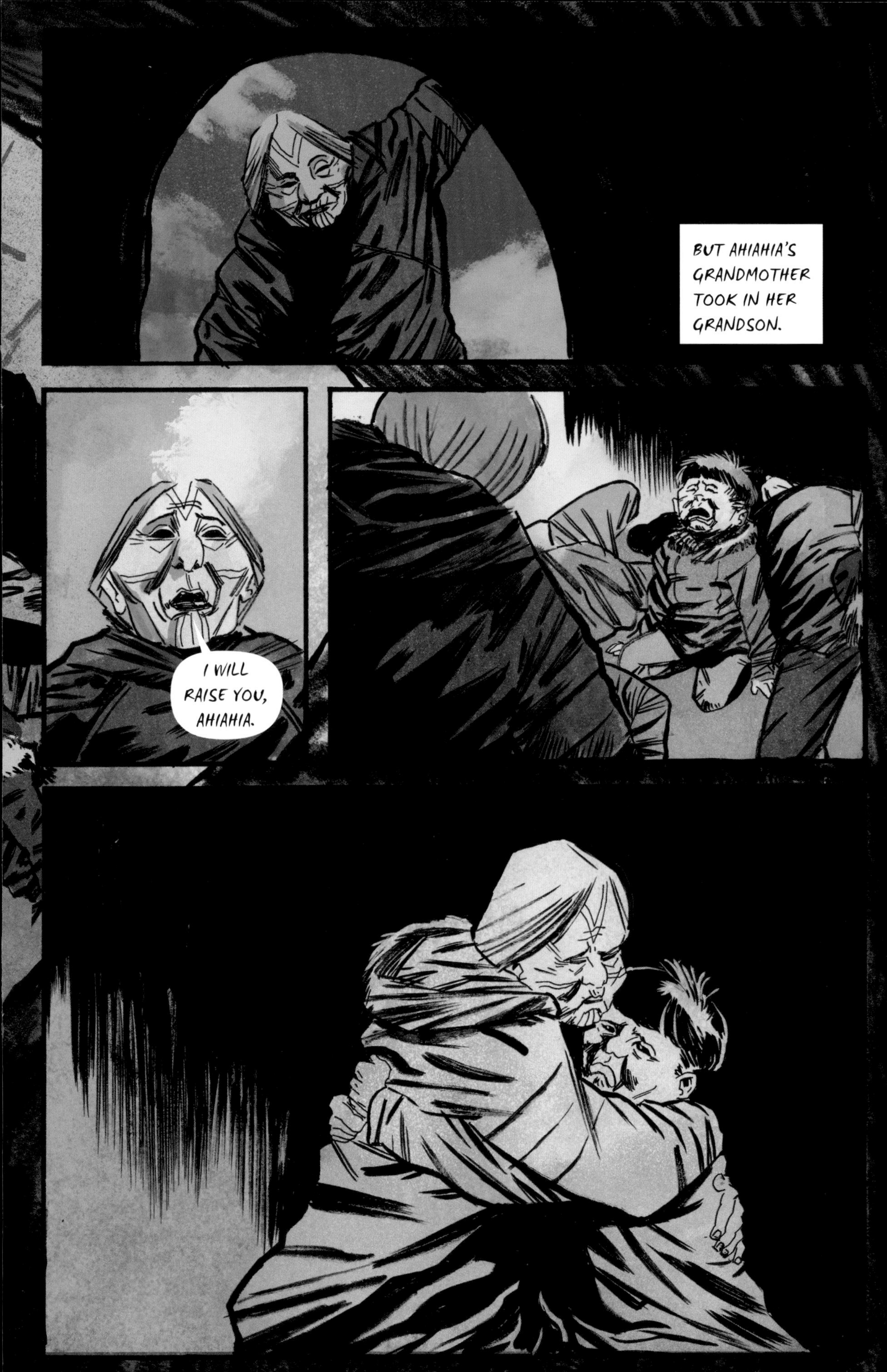
BUT AHIAHIA'S GRANDMOTHER TOOK IN HER GRANDSON.
I WILL RAISE YOU, AHIAHIA.

THE GRANDMOTHER RAISED AHIAHIA TO BE A STRONG YOUNG MAN.

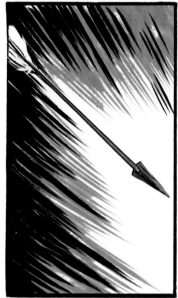

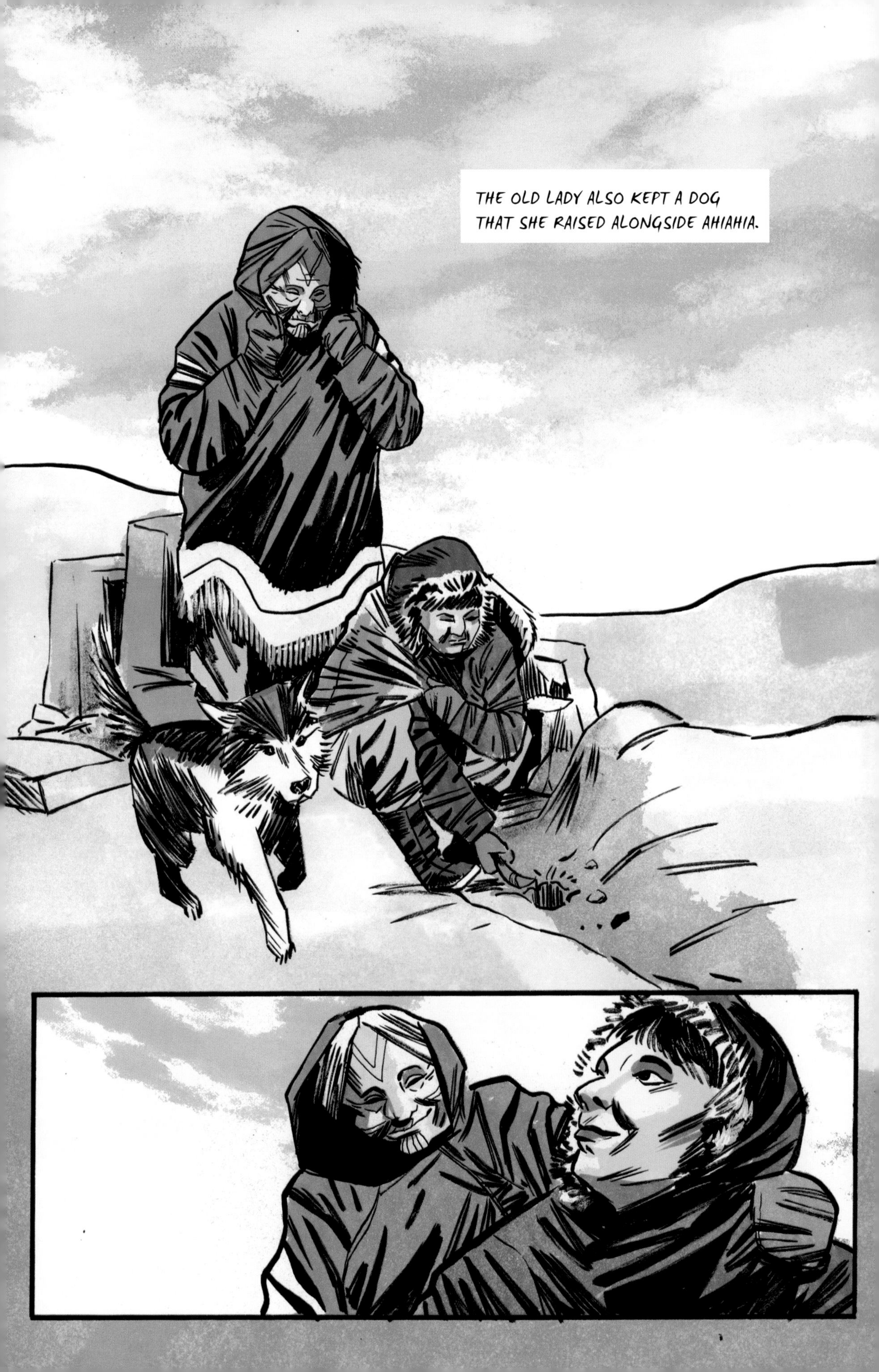
THE OLD LADY ALSO KEPT A DOG THAT SHE RAISED ALONGSIDE AHIAHIA.

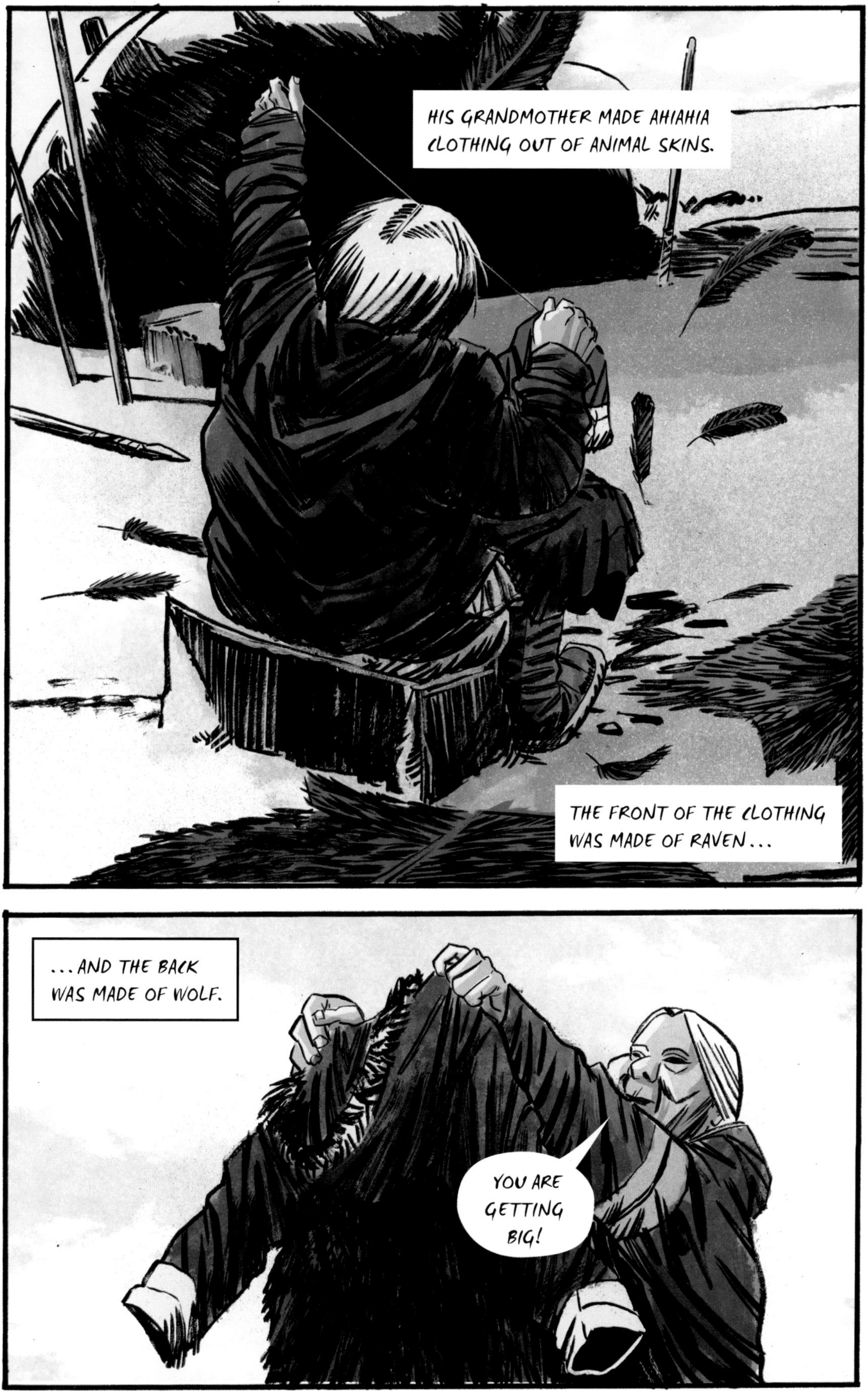
HIS GRANDMOTHER MADE AHIAHIA CLOTHING OUT OF ANIMAL SKINS.
THE FRONT OF THE CLOTHING WAS MADE OF RAVEN...
...AND THE BACK WAS MADE OF WOLF.
YOU ARE GETTING BIG!

HIS GRANDMOTHER ALSO MADE AMULETS AND A NECKLACE TO PROTECT AHIAHIA.

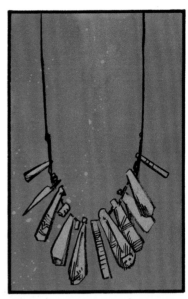

KEEP THESE CLOSE ALWAYS.

THESE WILL PROTECT ME FROM HARM.

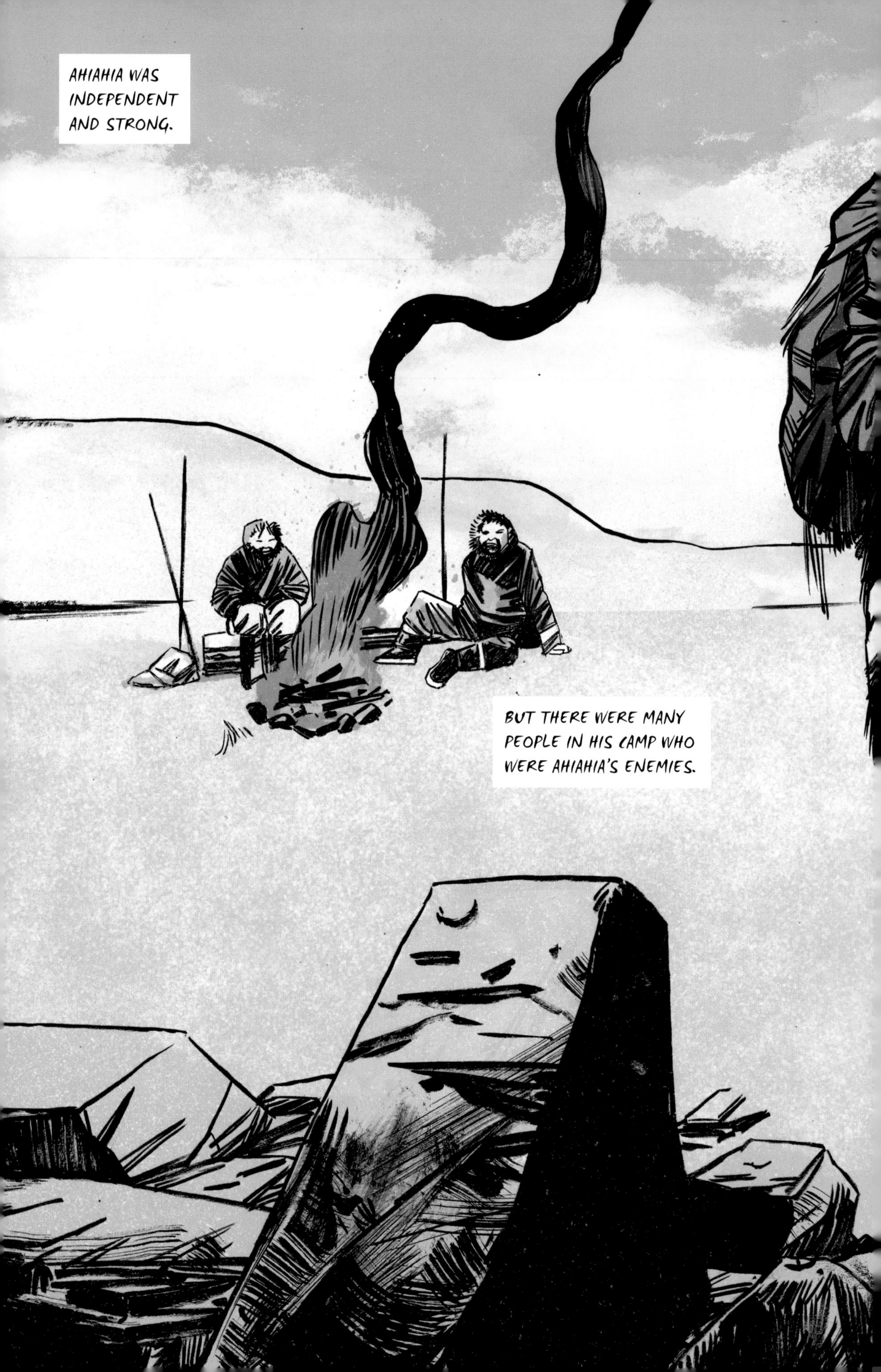
AHIAHIA WAS INDEPENDENT AND STRONG.
BUT THERE WERE MANY PEOPLE IN HIS CAMP WHO WERE AHIAHIA'S ENEMIES.

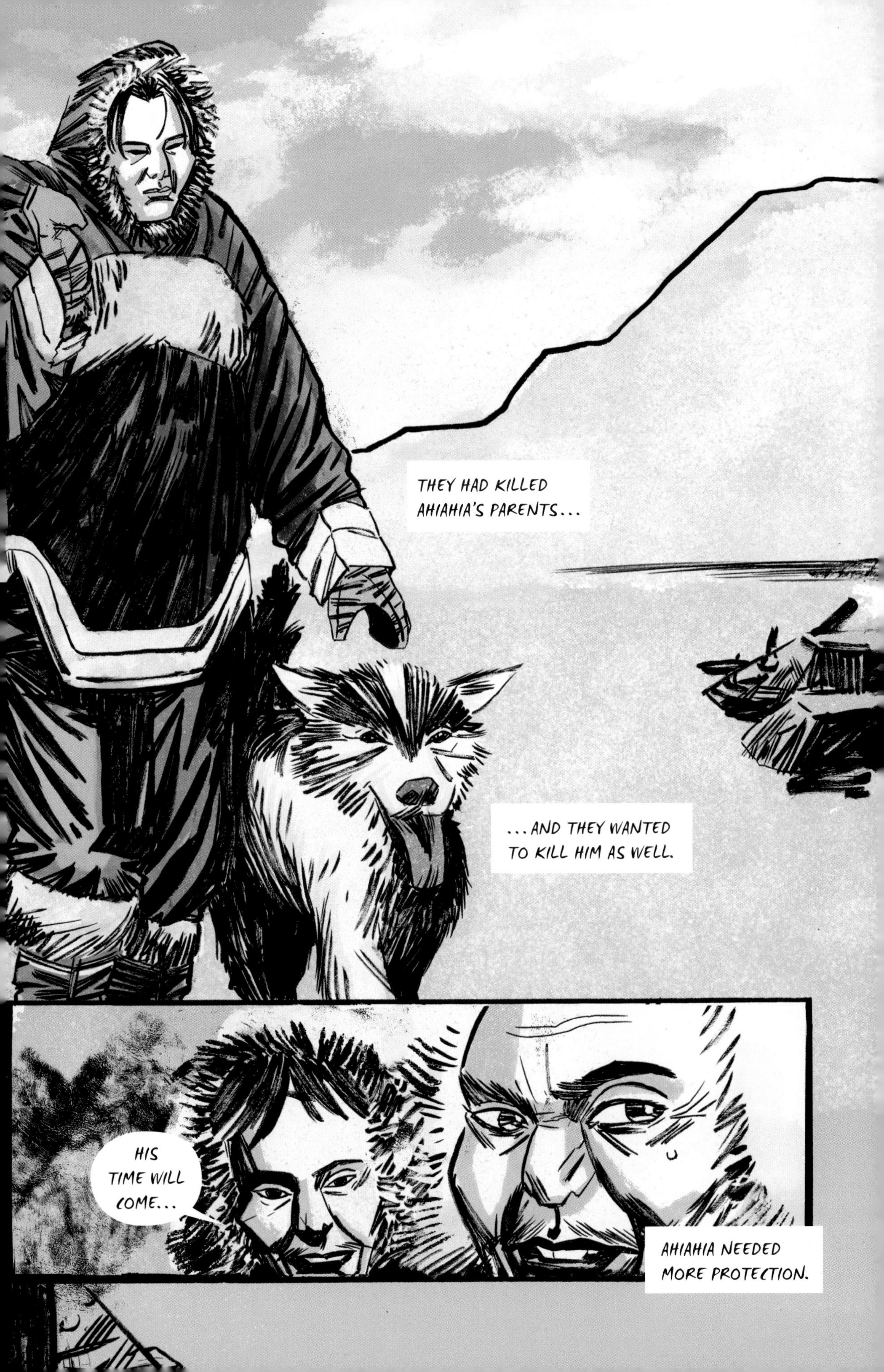
THEY HAD KILLED AHIAHIA'S PARENTS...
...AND THEY WANTED TO KILL HIM AS WELL.
HIS TIME WILL COME...
AHIAHIA NEEDED MORE PROTECTION.

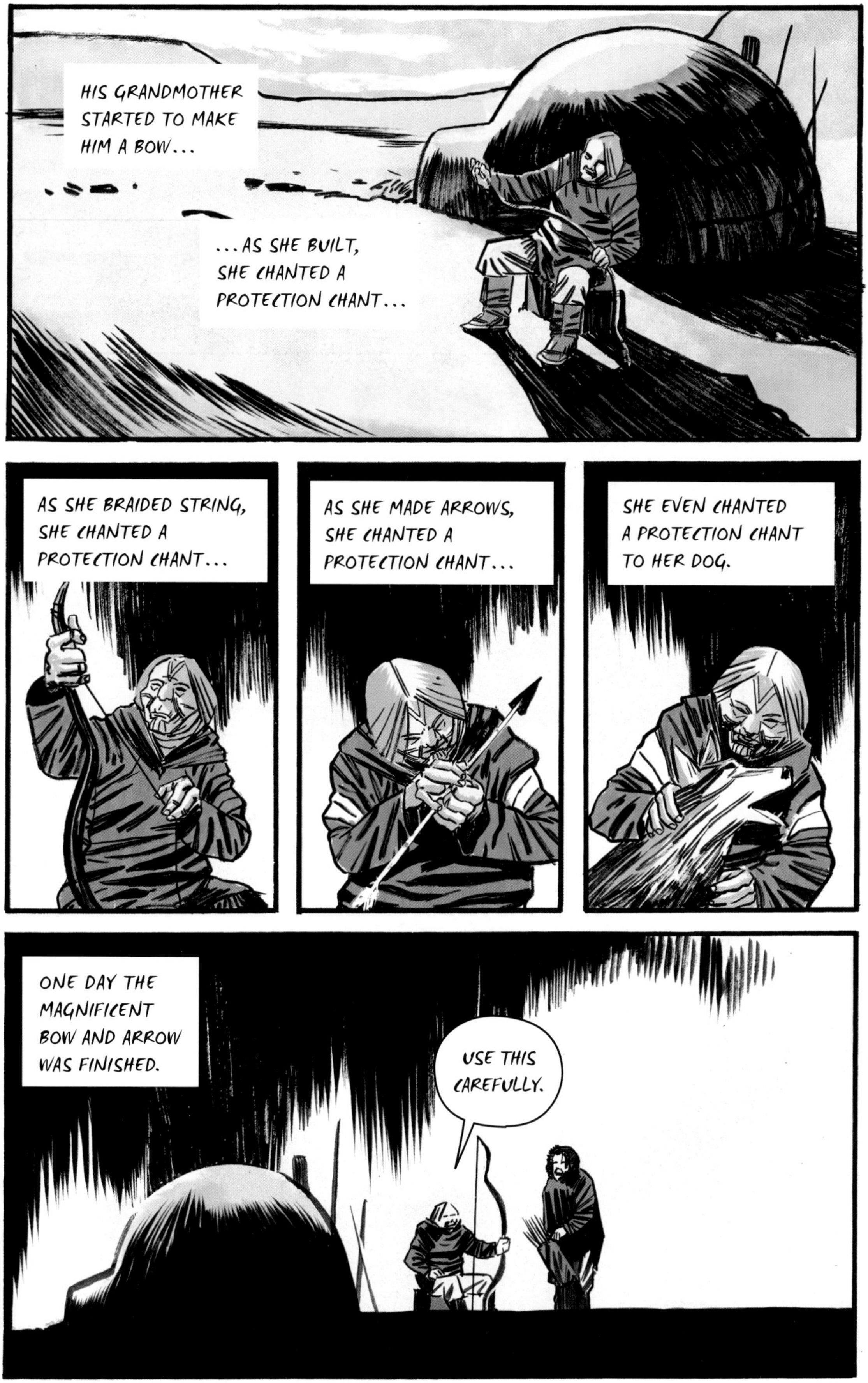
HIS GRANDMOTHER STARTED TO MAKE HIM A BOW...
...AS SHE BUILT, SHE CHANTED A PROTECTION CHANT...
AS SHE BRAIDED STRING, SHE CHANTED A PROTECTION CHANT...
AS SHE MADE ARROWS, SHE CHANTED A PROTECTION CHANT...
SHE EVEN CHANTED A PROTECTION CHANT TO HER DOG.
ONE DAY THE MAGNIFICENT BOW AND ARROW WAS FINISHED.
USE THIS CAREFULLY.

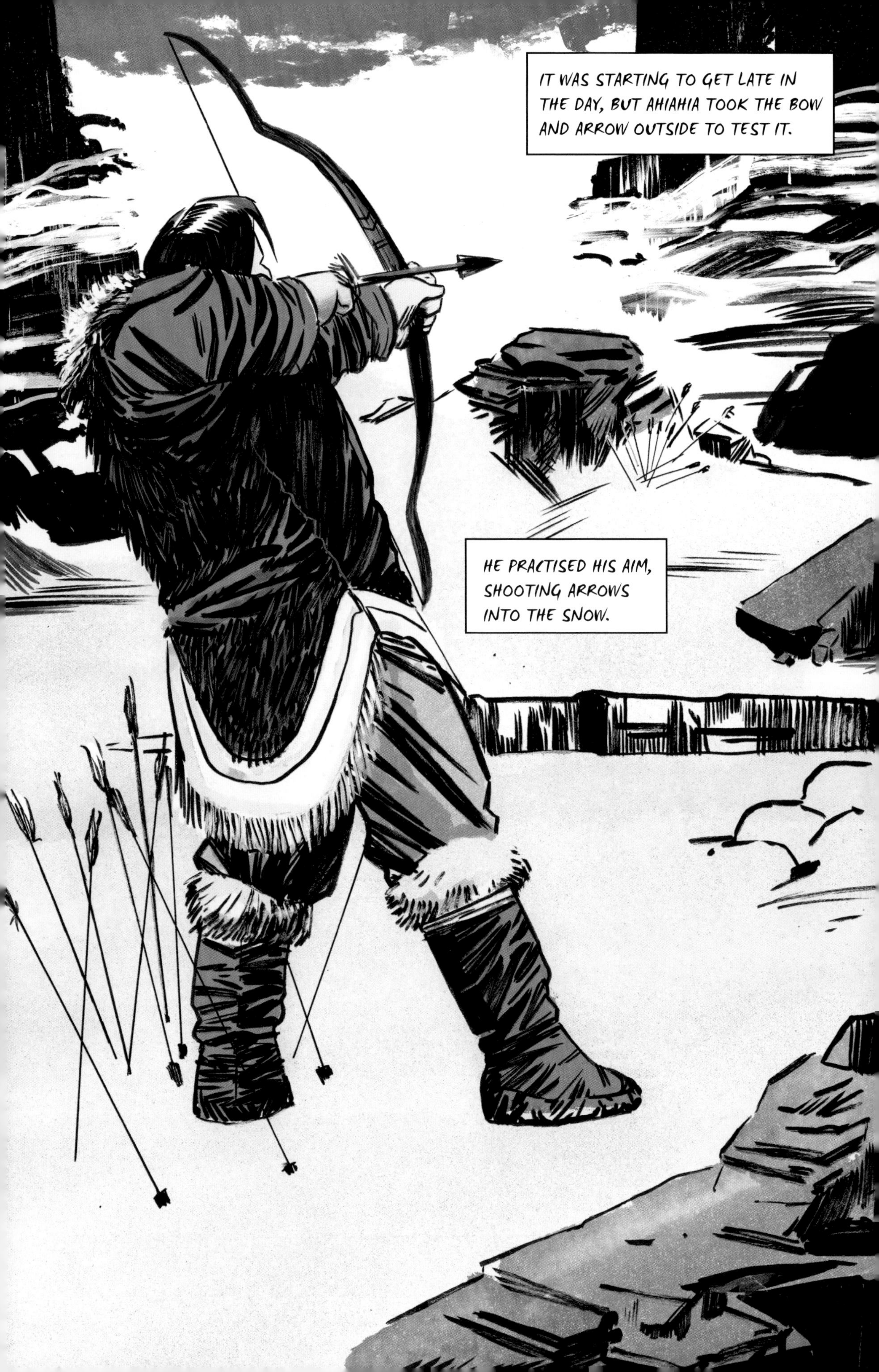
IT WAS STARTING TO GET LATE IN THE DAY, BUT AHIAHIA TOOK THE BOW AND ARROW OUTSIDE TO TEST IT.
HE PRACTISED HIS AIM, SHOOTING ARROWS INTO THE SNOW.

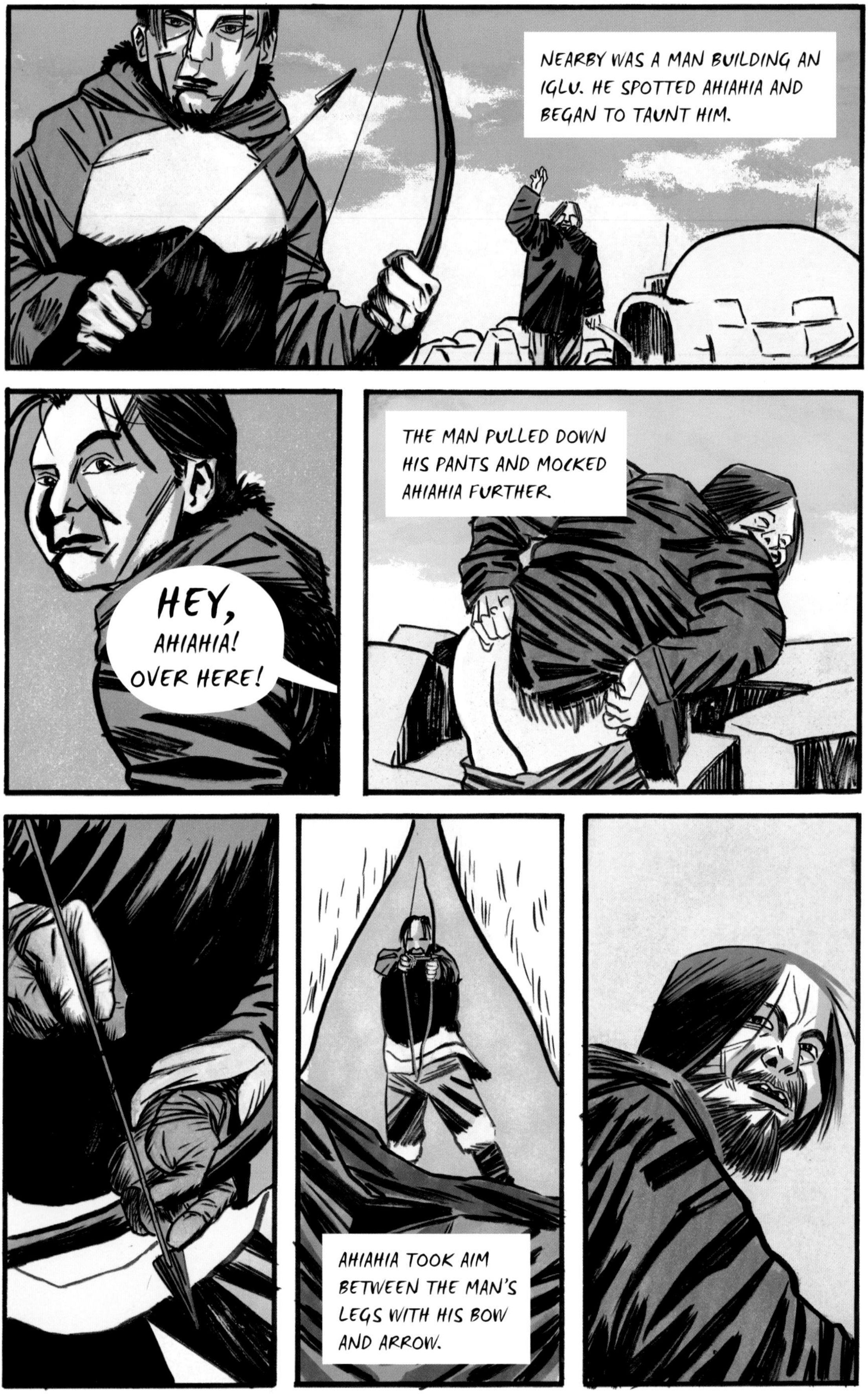
NEARBY WAS A MAN BUILDING AN IGLU. HE SPOTTED AHIAHIA AND BEGAN TO TAUNT HIM.
HEY, AHIAHIA! OVER HERE!
THE MAN PULLED DOWN HIS PANTS AND MOCKED AHIAHIA FURTHER.
AHIAHIA TOOK AIM BETWEEN THE MAN'S LEGS WITH HIS BOW AND ARROW.

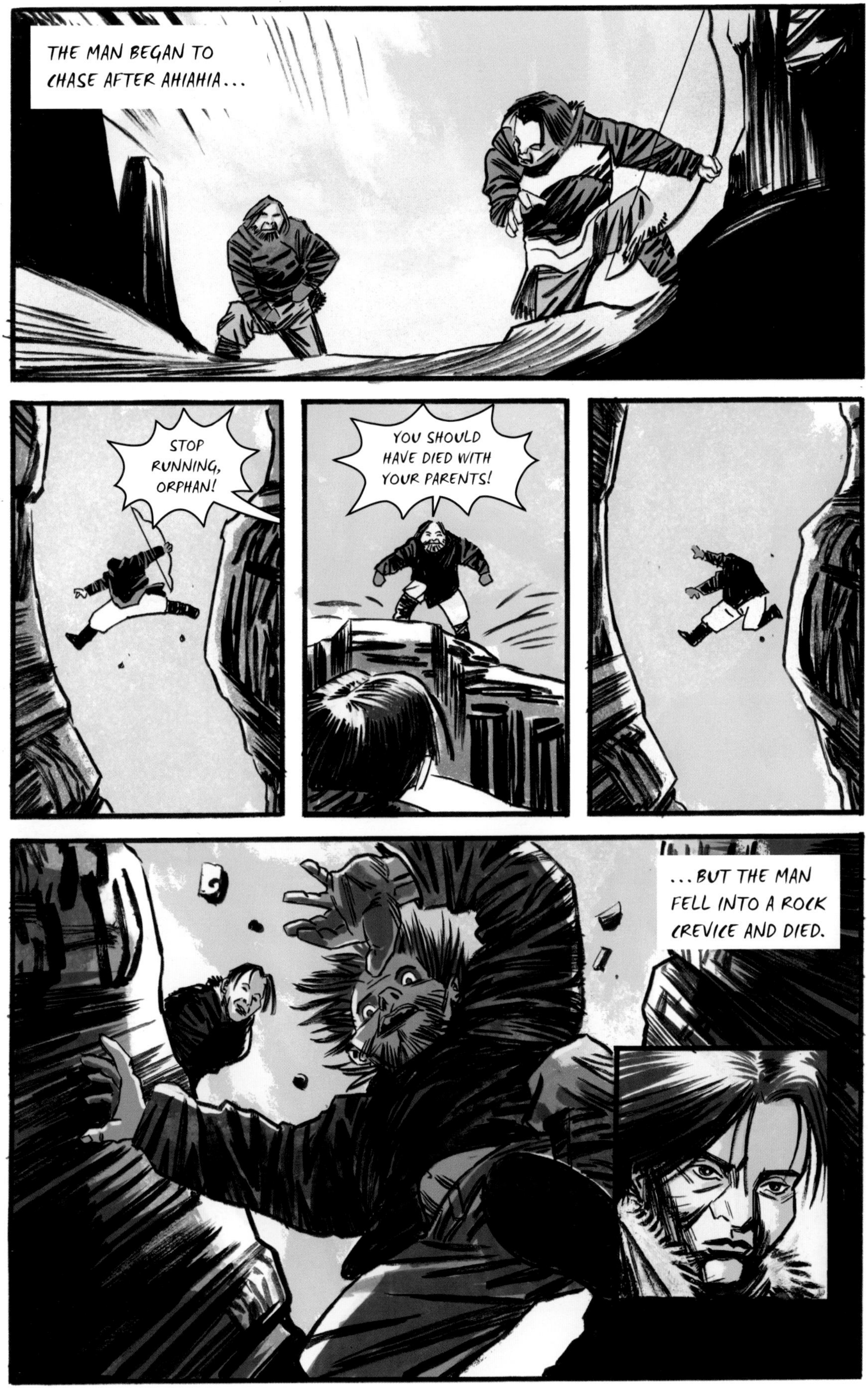
THE MAN BEGAN TO CHASE AFTER AHIAHIA...
STOP RUNNING, ORPHAN!
YOU SHOULD HAVE DIED WITH YOUR PARENTS!
...BUT THE MAN FELL INTO A ROCK CREVICE AND DIED.

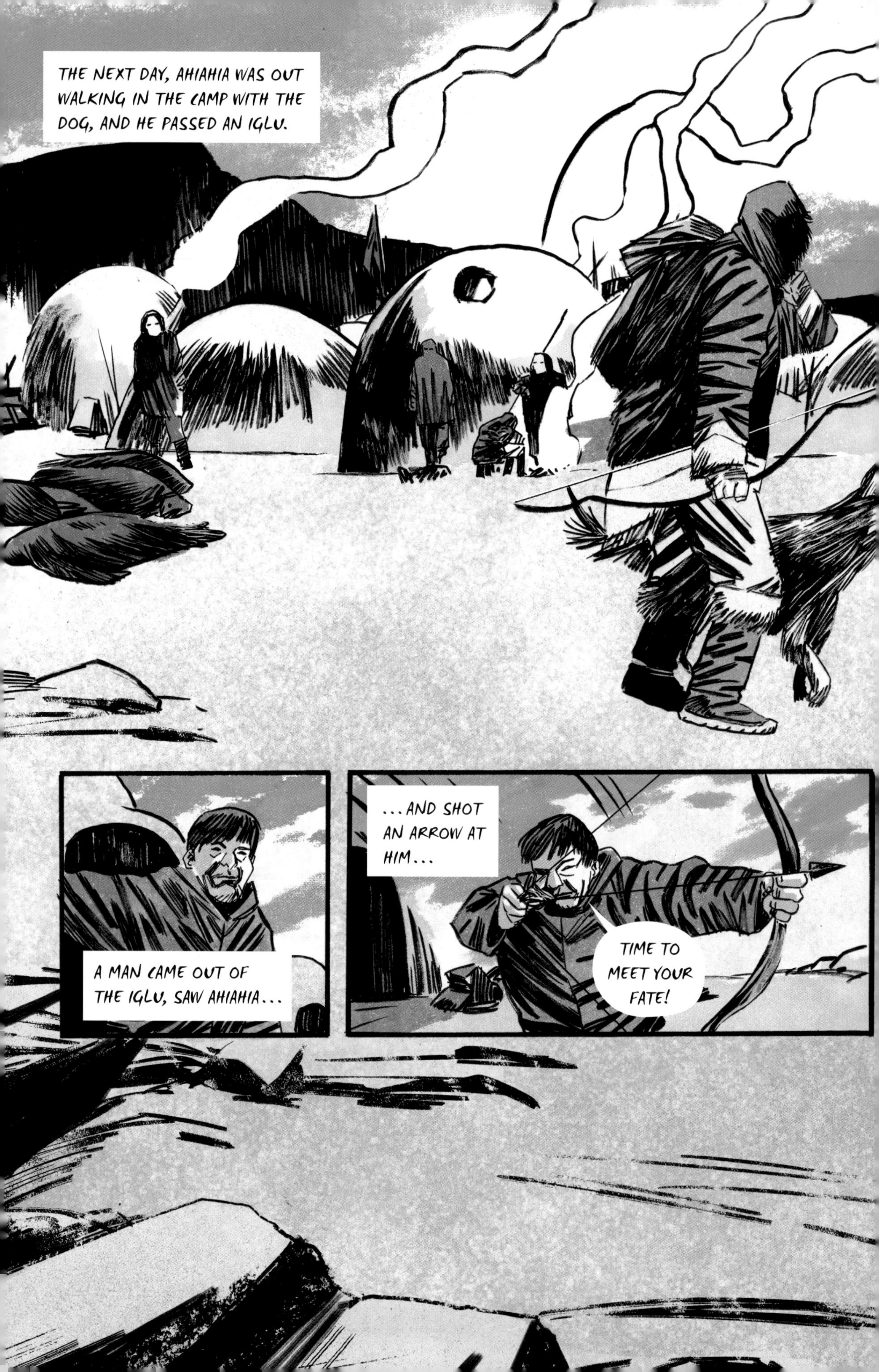
THE NEXT DAY, AHIAHIA WAS OUT WALKING IN THE CAMP WITH THE DOG, AND HE PASSED AN IGLU.
A MAN CAME OUT OF THE IGLU, SAW AHIAHIA...
...AND SHOT AN ARROW AT HIM...
TIME TO MEET YOUR FATE!

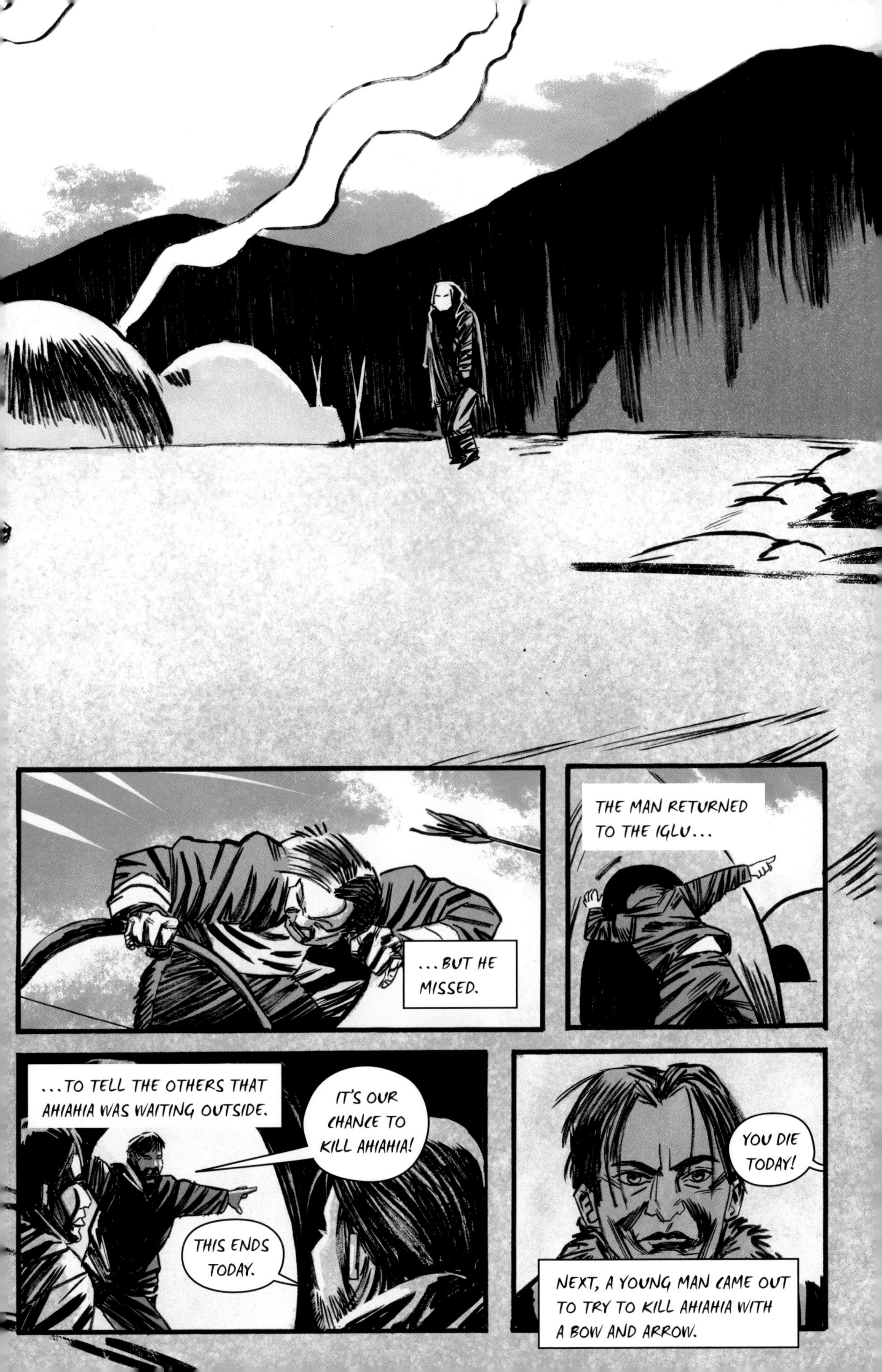
...BUT HE MISSED.
THE MAN RETURNED TO THE IGLU...
...TO TELL THE OTHERS THAT AHIAHIA WAS WAITING OUTSIDE.
IT'S OUR CHANCE TO KILL AHIAHIA!
THIS ENDS TODAY.
NEXT, A YOUNG MAN CAME OUT TO TRY TO KILL AHIAHIA WITH A BOW AND ARROW.
YOU DIE TODAY!

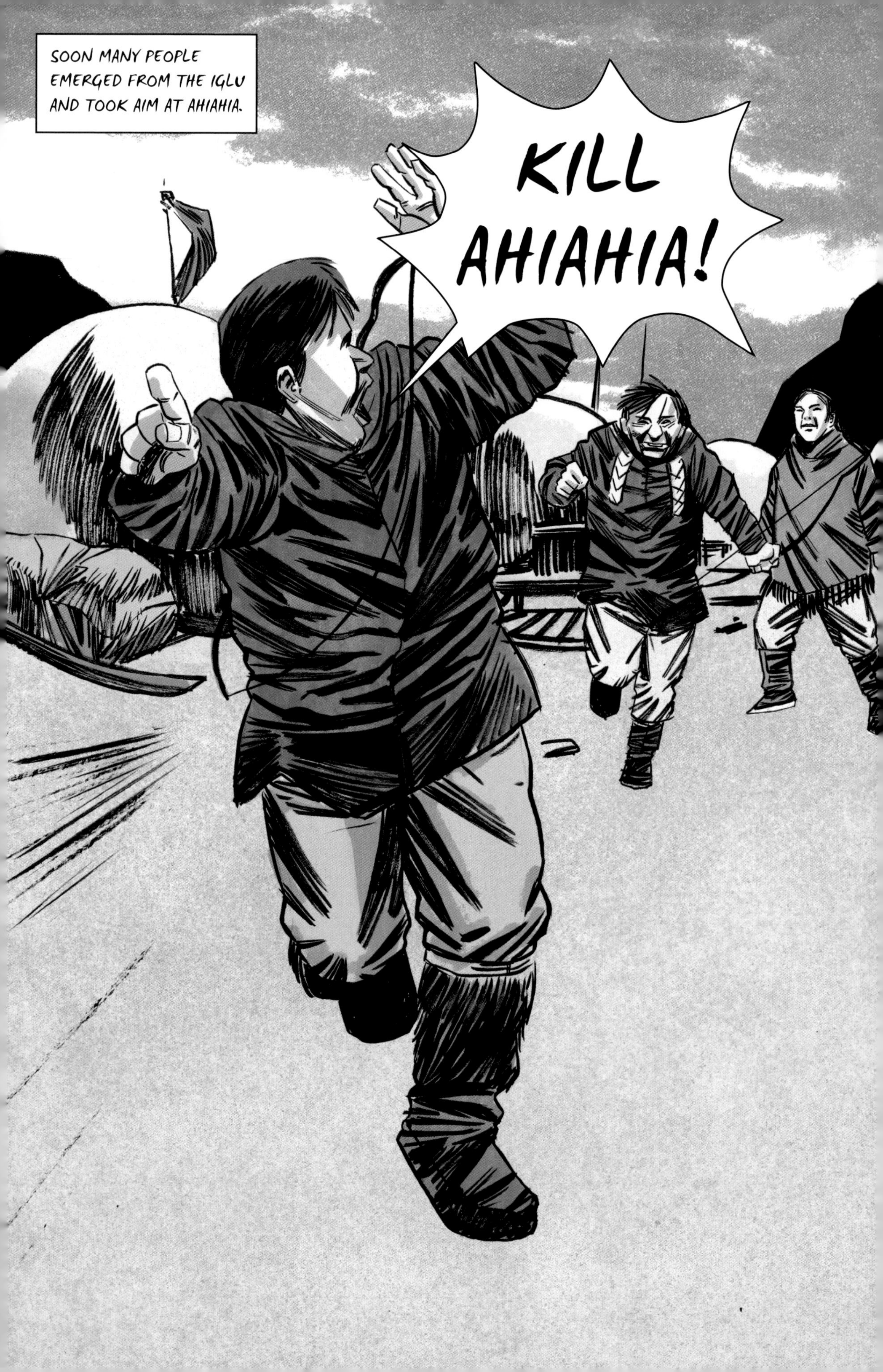
SOON MANY PEOPLE EMERGED FROM THE IGLU AND TOOK AIM AT AHIAHIA.
KILL AHIAHIA!

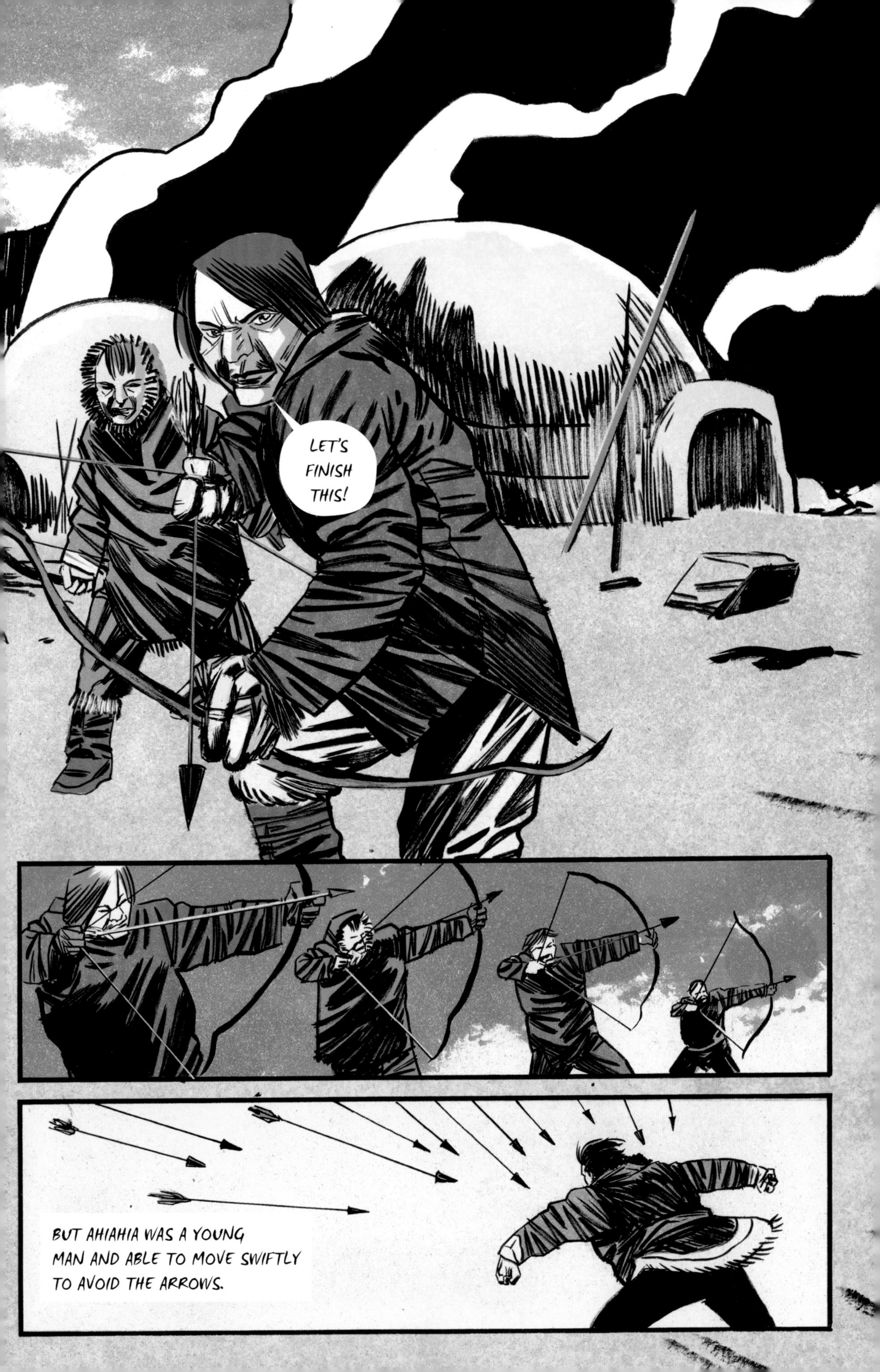
LET'S FINISH THIS!
BUT AHIAHIA WAS A YOUNG MAN AND ABLE TO MOVE SWIFTLY TO AVOID THE ARROWS.

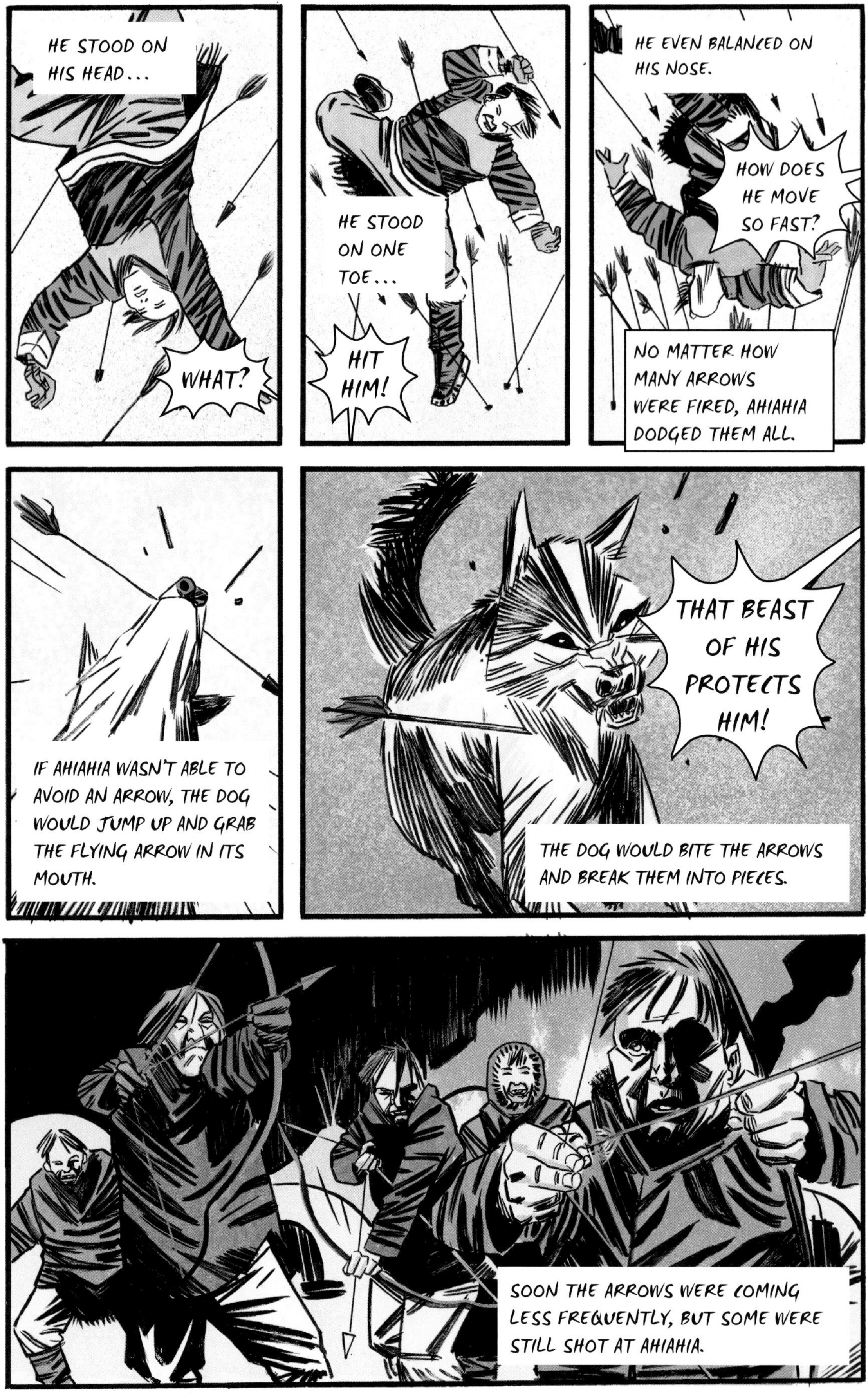
HE STOOD ON HIS HEAD...
WHAT?
HE STOOD ON ONE TOE...
HIT HIM!
HE EVEN BALANCED ON HIS NOSE.
HOW DOES HE MOVE SO FAST?
NO MATTER HOW MANY ARROWS WERE FIRED, AHIAHIA DODGED THEM ALL.
IF AHIAHIA WASN'T ABLE TO AVOID AN ARROW, THE DOG WOULD JUMP UP AND GRAB THE FLYING ARROW IN ITS MOUTH.
THAT BEAST OF HIS PROTECTS HIM!
THE DOG WOULD BITE THE ARROWS AND BREAK THEM INTO PIECES.
SOON THE ARROWS WERE COMING LESS FREQUENTLY, BUT SOME WERE STILL SHOT AT AHIAHIA.

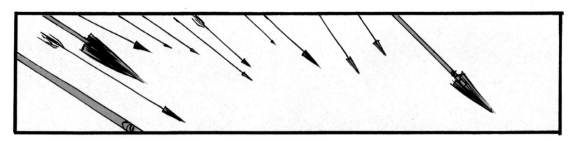

SOME HIT HIM ON HIS FRONT, MAKING A RAVEN SOUND.

CAW

CAW

CAW

SOME HIT HIM ON HIS BACK, MAKING A WOLF SOUND.

AWOO

AWOO

AWOO

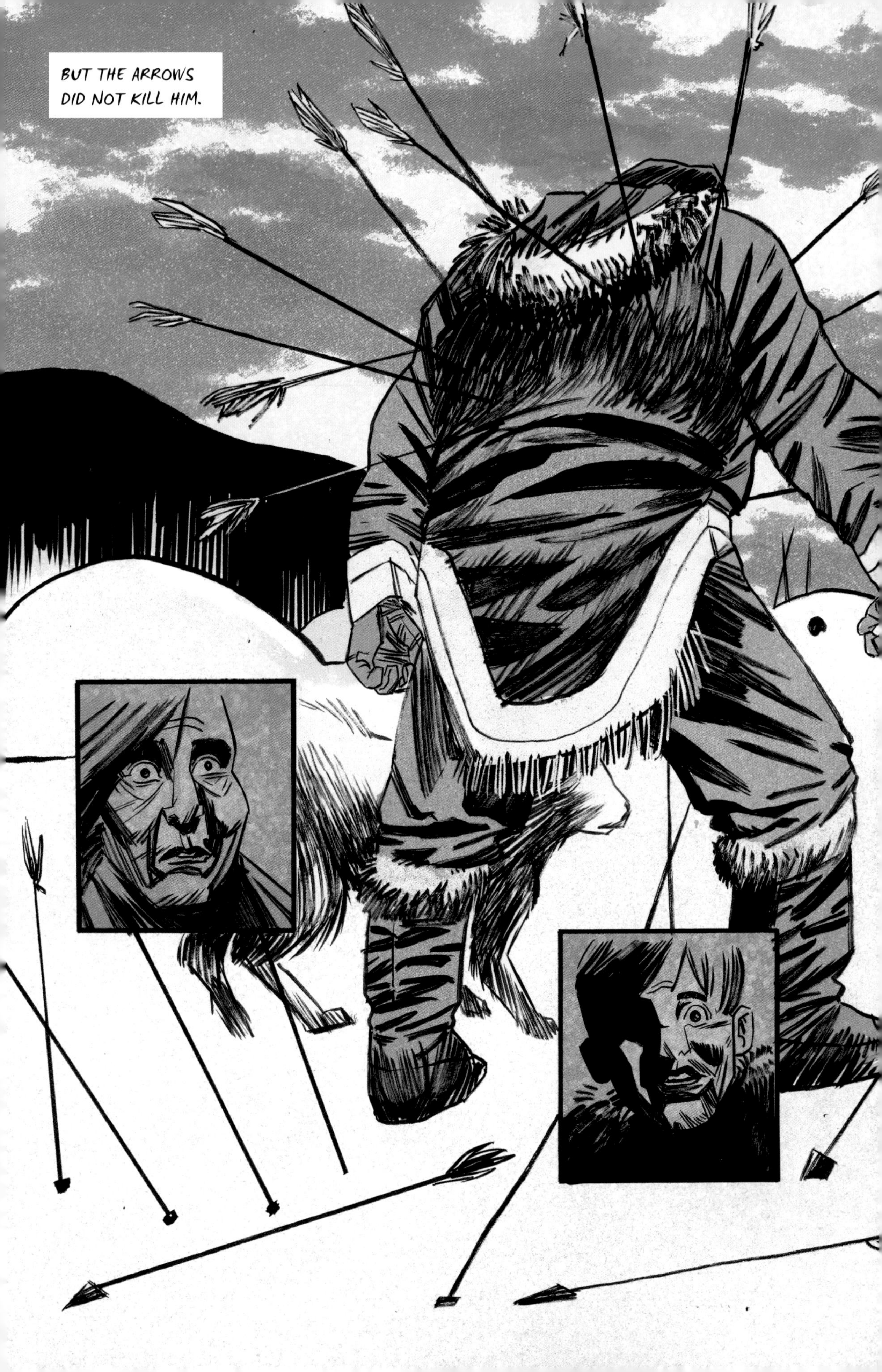
BUT THE ARROWS DID NOT KILL HIM.

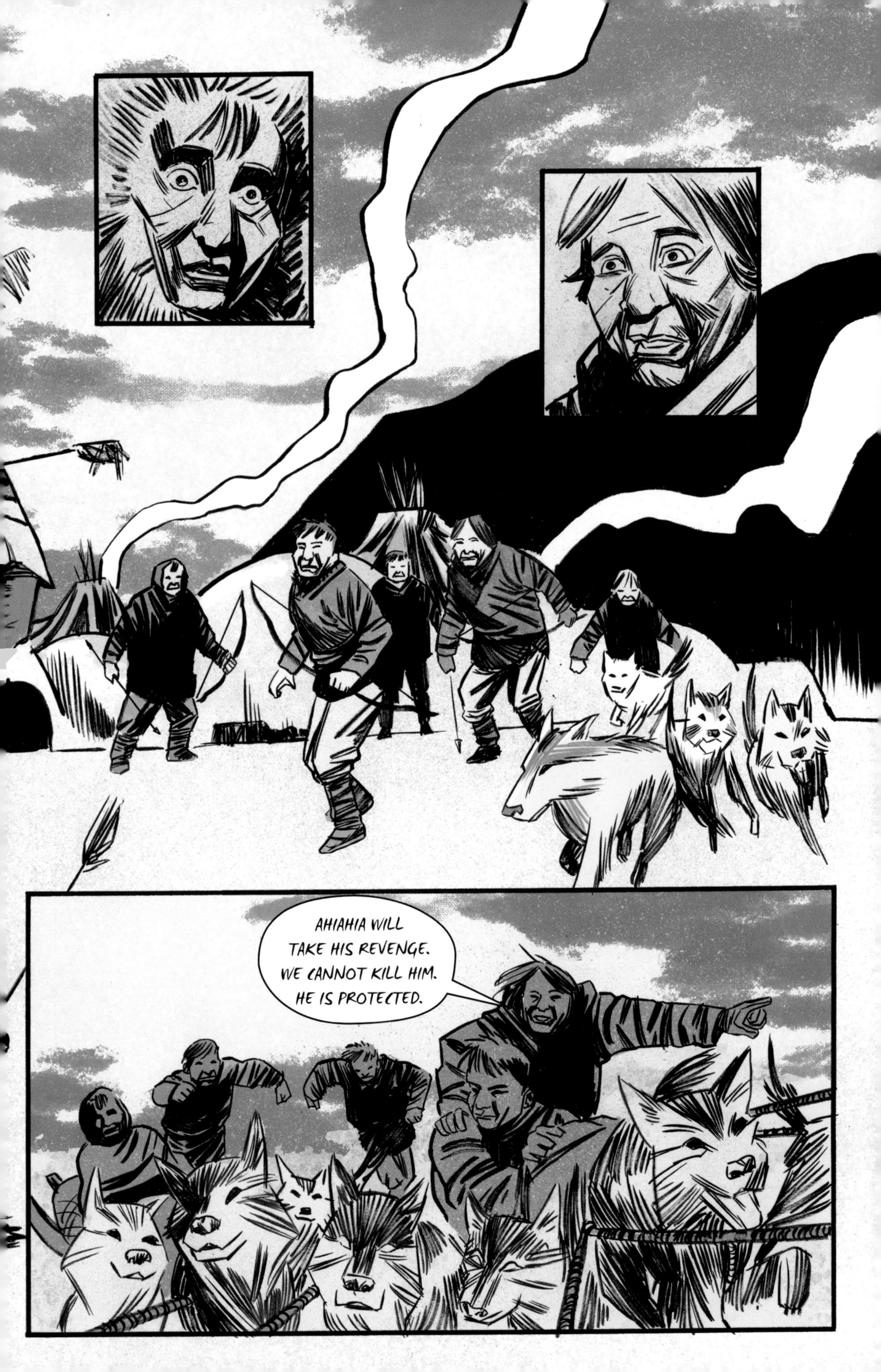
AHIAHIA WILL TAKE HIS REVENGE. WE CANNOT KILL HIM. HE IS PROTECTED.

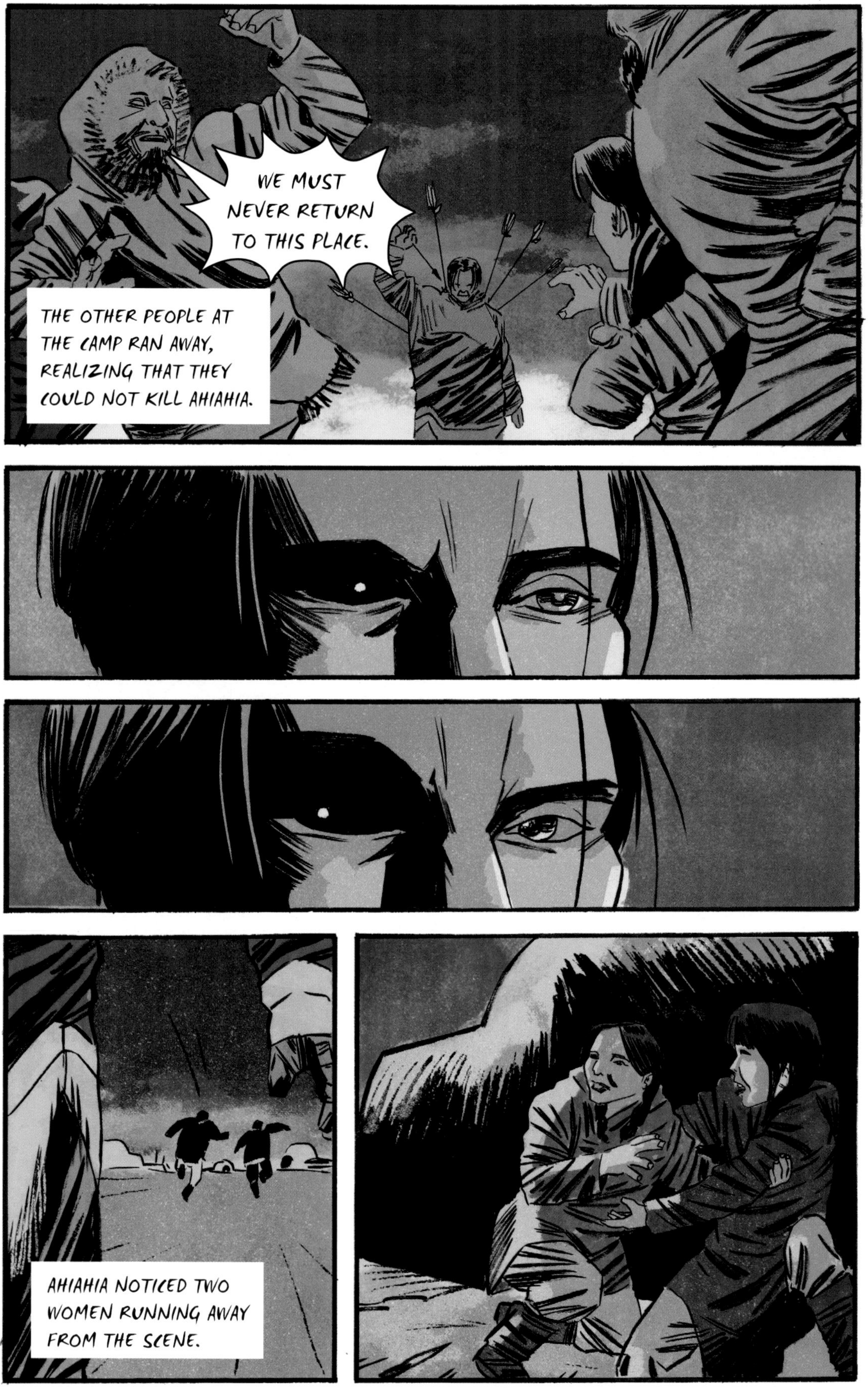
WE MUST NEVER RETURN TO THIS PLACE.
THE OTHER PEOPLE AT THE CAMP RAN AWAY, REALIZING THAT THEY COULD NOT KILL AHIAHIA.
AHIAHIA NOTICED TWO WOMEN RUNNING AWAY FROM THE SCENE.

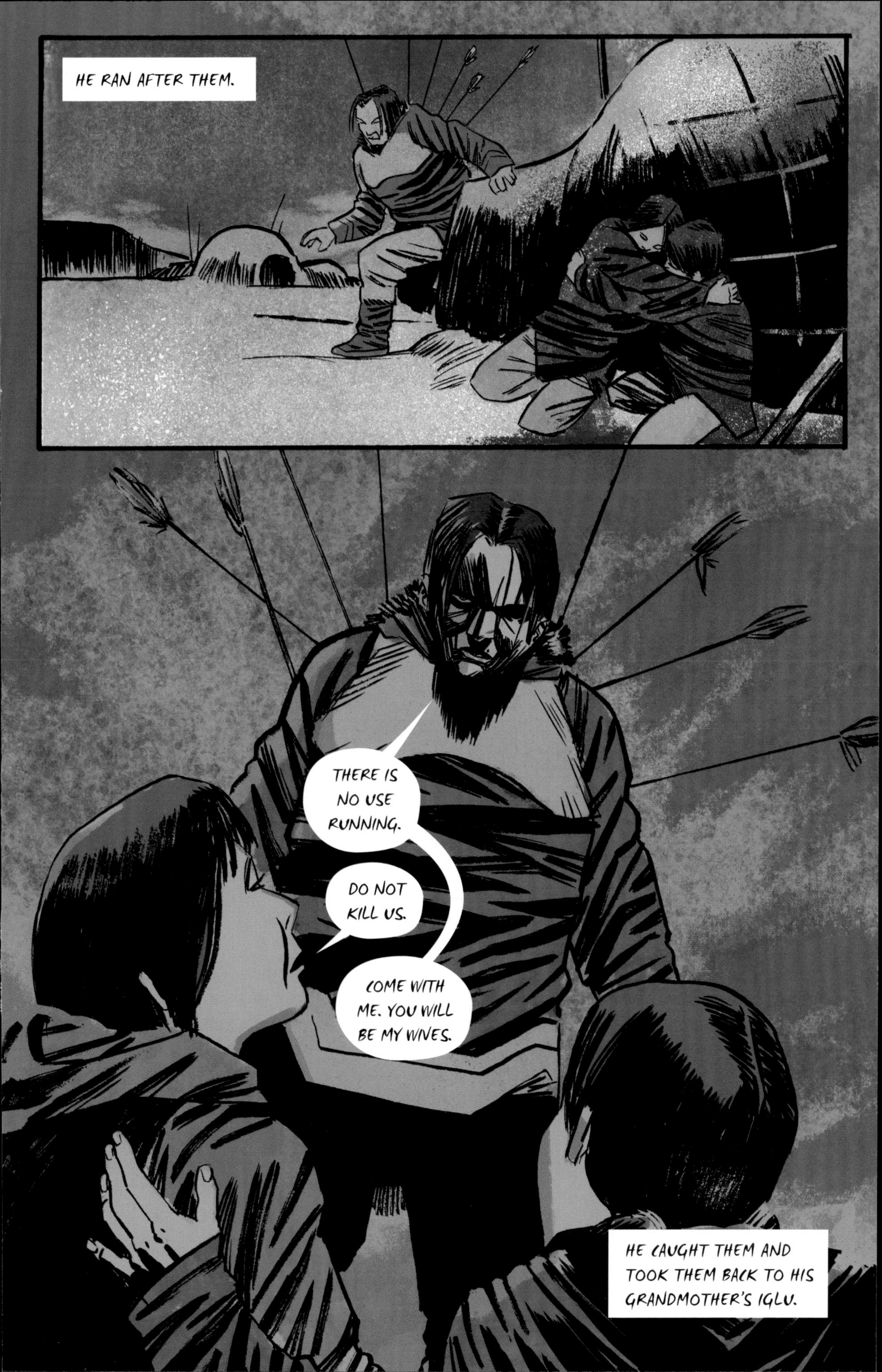
HE RAN AFTER THEM.
THERE IS NO USE RUNNING.
DO NOT KILL US.
COME WITH ME. YOU WILL BE MY WIVES.
HE CAUGHT THEM AND TOOK THEM BACK TO HIS GRANDMOTHER'S IGLU.

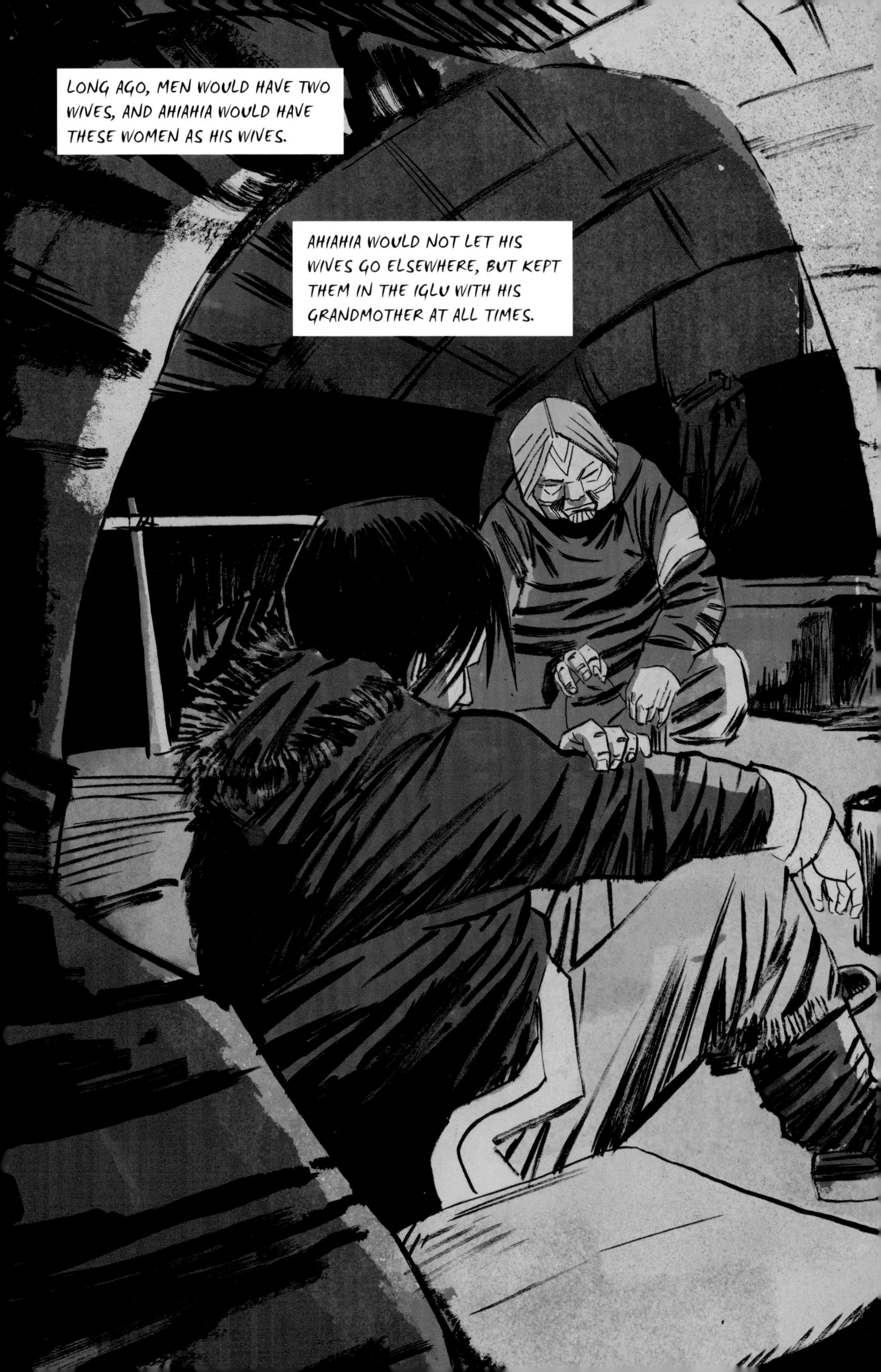
LONG AGO, MEN WOULD HAVE TWO WIVES, AND AHIAHIA WOULD HAVE THESE WOMEN AS HIS WIVES.
AHIAHIA WOULD NOT LET HIS WIVES GO ELSEWHERE, BUT KEPT THEM IN THE IGLU WITH HIS GRANDMOTHER AT ALL TIMES.

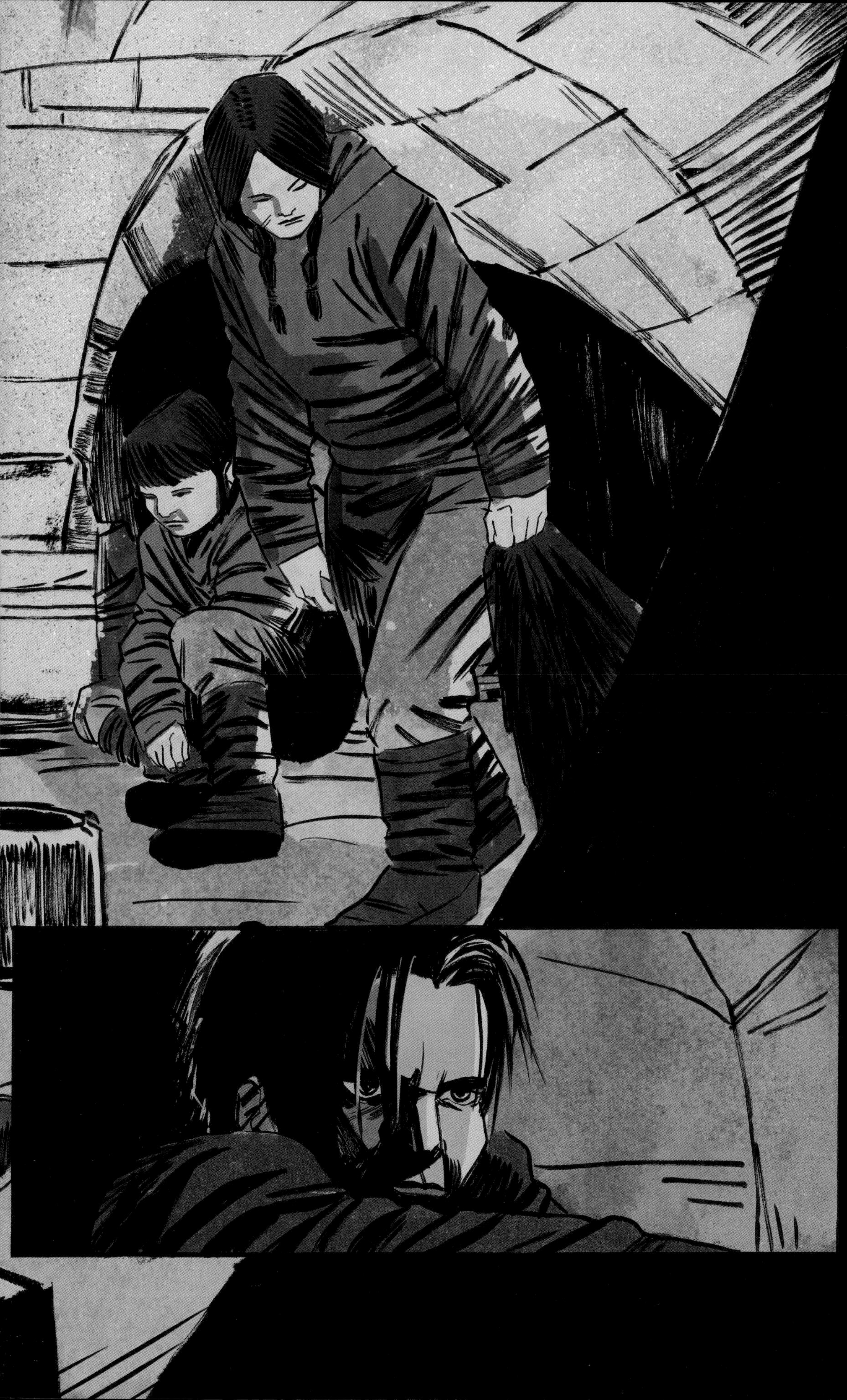

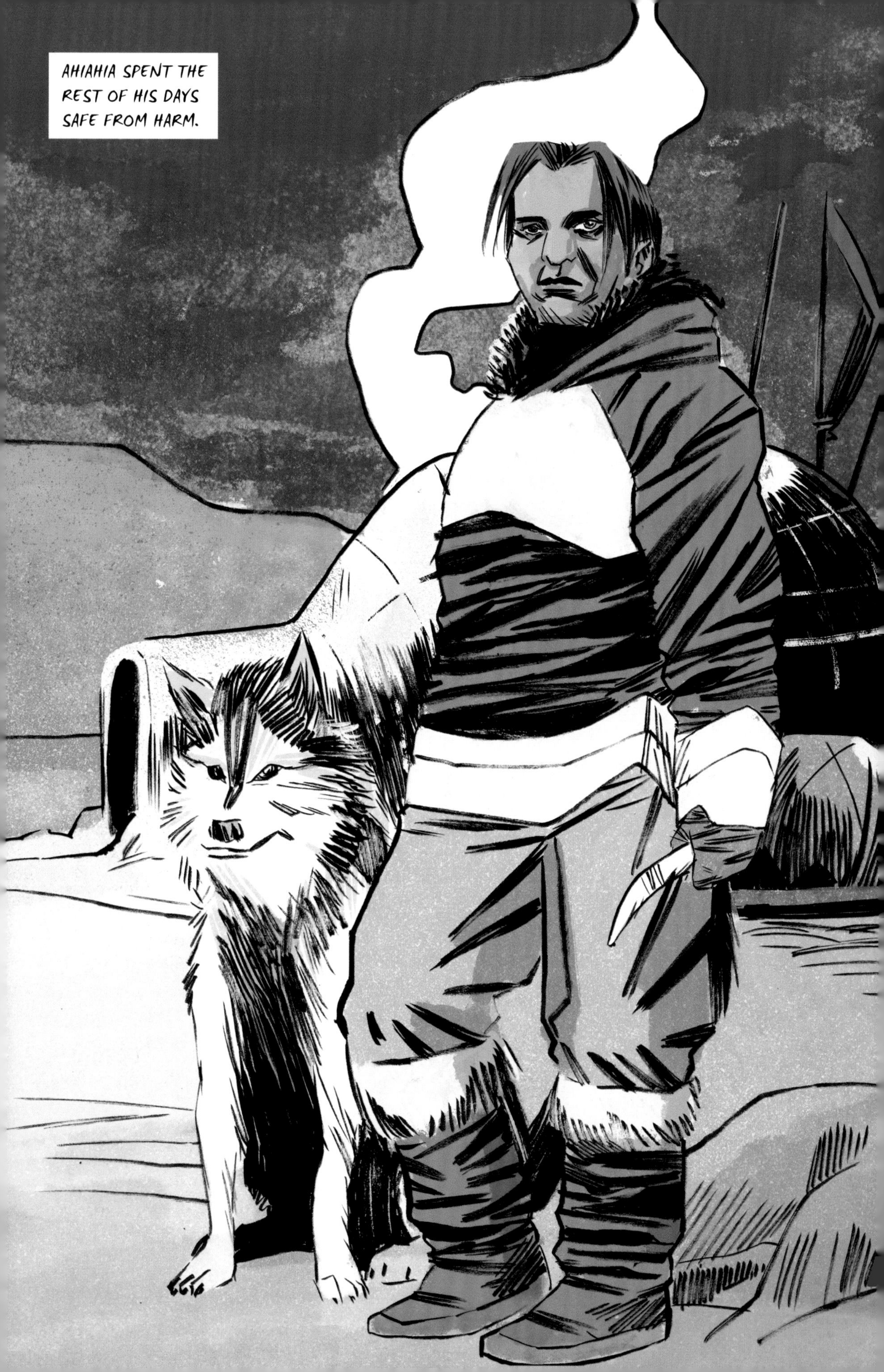
AHIAHIA SPENT THE REST OF HIS DAYS SAFE FROM HARM.

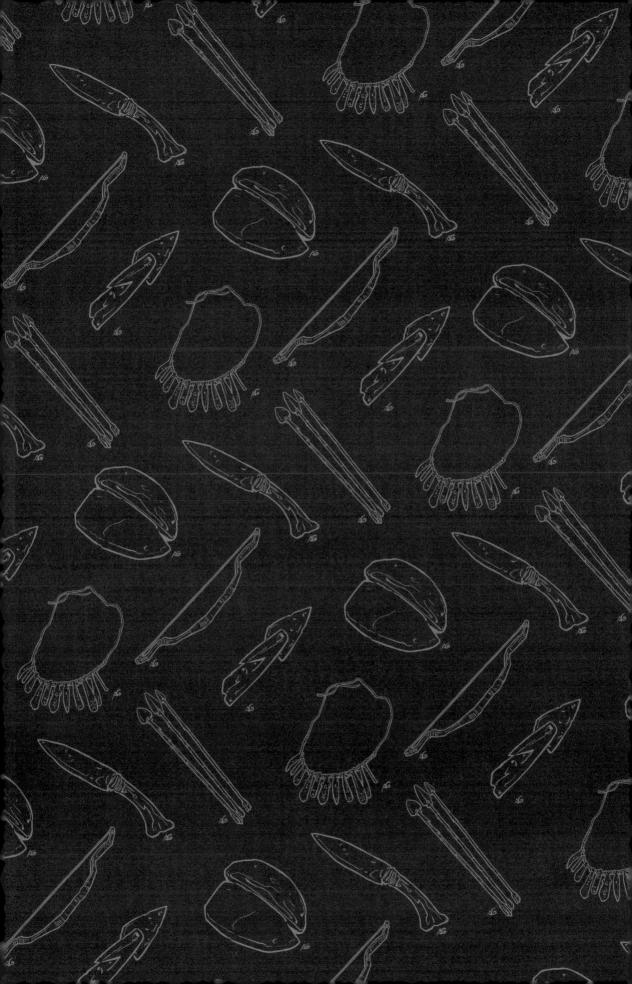

Levi Illuitok was born in Qilijauqtuaq, Kugaaruk, a community in Nunavut. While growing up, he and his family travelled by land and didn't stay in one place for long. Levi enjoys going out on the land and hunting. He also teaches his traditional knowledge to students.

Nate Wells is an illustrator and designer living in Texas. While studying graphic design at Texas Tech University, Nate began his career in cartooning at the school's newspaper, *The Daily Toreador*, where he worked as an editorial cartoonist. Nate now works in the fields of comic books, film, and music, creating posters, sequential art, and concept art.

Glossary of Inuktut Words

Inuktut is the word for Inuit languages spoken in Canada, including Inuktitut and Inuinnaqtun. The pronunciation guides in this book are intended to support non-Inuktut speakers in their reading of Inuktut words. These pronunciations are not exact representations of how the words are pronounced by Inuktut speakers. For more resources on how to pronounce Inuktut words, visit inhabitmedia.com/inuitnipingit.

Inuktut term	Pronunciation	Meaning
Ahiahia	ah-HEEAH-heeah	name
iglu	EE-gloo	a snow house

INHABIT
MEDIA

IQALUIT · TORONTO

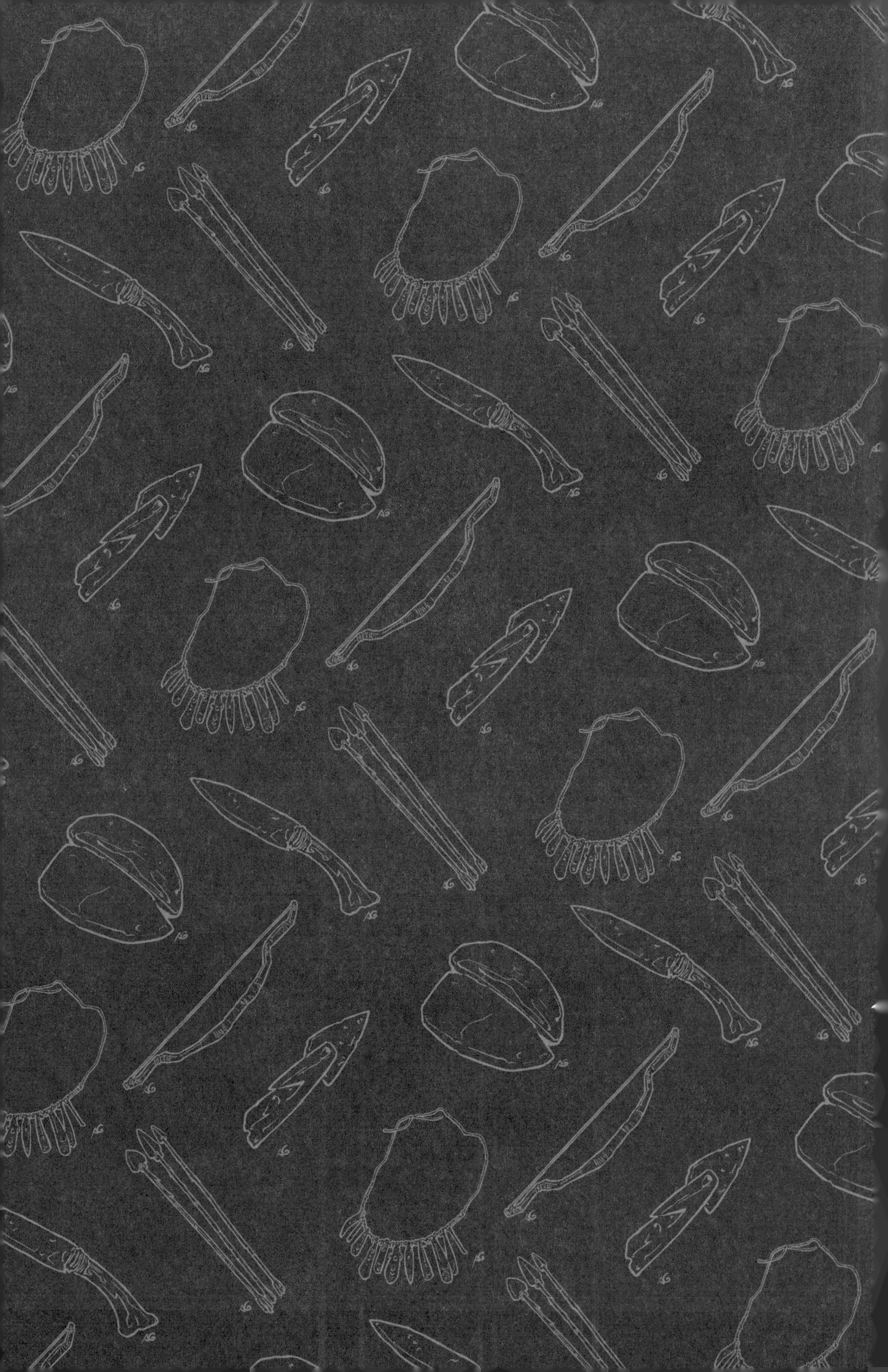